DEAD MAN WALKING

"If you don't stop, I'll shoot you in the leg," Fargo warned. The Colt leaped into his hand, but before he could shoot, the speckled apparition sprang with surprising speed. Barely in time, Fargo skipped aside. He found himself with his back to a stall, and the way out cut off.

The man's waxen features contorted, but whether in a grimace or a grin, Fargo couldn't say.

Suddenly light flooded the barn. Russ Cepna had opened the door all the way and was saying, "What's taking so long—" Catching sight of the man, he blurted, "Byerly! What in God's name?"

The living nightmare turned toward the farmer. Curling his fingers like talons, Byerly lurched toward him.

"Byerly, no!" Russ skipped backward, or tried to. He tripped and fell to one knee.

The thing called Byerly was almost on him when a shotgun blasted. . . .

THE TRAILSMAN

#306

NEBRASKA
NIGHT RIDERS

by

Jon Sharpe

A SIGNET BOOK

SIGNET
Published by New American Library, a division of
Penguin Group (USA) Inc., 375 Hudson Street,
New York, New York 10014, USA
Penguin Group (Canada), 90 Eglinton Avenue East, Suite 700, Toronto,
Ontario M4P 2Y3, Canada (a division of Pearson Penguin Canada Inc.)
Penguin Books Ltd., 80 Strand, London WC2R 0RL, England
Penguin Ireland, 25 St. Stephen's Green, Dublin 2,
Ireland (a division of Penguin Books Ltd.)
Penguin Group (Australia), 250 Camberwell Road, Camberwell, Victoria 3124,
Australia (a division of Pearson Australia Group Pty. Ltd.)
Penguin Books India Pvt. Ltd., 11 Community Centre, Panchsheel Park,
New Delhi - 110 017, India
Penguin Group (NZ), 67 Apollo Drive, Mairangi Bay,
Auckland 1311, New Zealand (a division of Pearson New Zealand Ltd.)
Penguin Books (South Africa) (Pty.) Ltd., 24 Sturdee Avenue,
Rosebank, Johannesburg 2196, South Africa

Penguin Books Ltd., Registered Offices:
80 Strand, London WC2R 0RL, England

First published by Signet, an imprint of New American Library,
a division of Penguin Group (USA) Inc.

First Printing, April 2007
10 9 8 7 6 5 4 3 2 1

The first chapter of this book previously appeared in *Wyoming Wipeout*, the three
hundred fifth volume in this series.

The Trailsman

Beginnings . . . they bend the tree and they mark the man. Skye Fargo was born when he was eighteen. Terror was his midwife, vengeance his first cry. Killing spawned Skye Fargo, ruthless, cold-blooded murder. Out of the acrid smoke of gunpowder still hanging in the air, he rose, cried out a promise never forgotten.

The Trailsman they began to call him all across the West: searcher, scout, hunter, the man who could see where others only looked, his skills for hire but not his soul, the man who lived each day to the fullest, yet trailed each tomorrow. Skye Fargo, the Trailsman, the seeker who could take the wildness of a land and the wanting of a woman and make them his own.

Nebraska Territory, 1861—
where hooded vigilantes and a
virulent disease made for a deadly combination.

1

Smoke sparked the rider's interest.

A big man clad in buckskins, he wore a white hat caked with so much dust it was almost brown. A red bandanna was around his neck. Broad of shoulder, slim of waist, the most striking aspect was his lake blue eyes. Piercing eyes that missed nothing. He sat the saddle of his Ovaro with an ease that hinted he was as much a part of the wide-open spaces as the mountains and the prairies.

Skye Fargo was his name. Scout, tracker, frontiersman, he was called all those, and one thing more. Throughout the untamed land he called home, he was known far and wide as the Trailsman.

On this sunny morning Fargo was on his way east. He was bound for St. Louis, the gateway to the West. A bustling, rowdy, lecherous beehive, with more saloons and taverns than any city between the Mississippi and San Francisco. A city as raw and wild as the unexplored vastness that lay beyond it. A city where a man like Fargo could indulge his passions for whiskey, women, and cards to his heart's content. He could not wait get there.

Fargo was not quite midway between Fort Laramie and Fort Kearney, headed east, following a rutted ribbon south of the Platte River. A ribbon that was in fact the main trail linking St. Louis with the far-distant Oregon Country.

The smoke was up ahead. The reason it perked Fargo's

interest was that it was not the usual gray of campfire smoke. It was black, which told him something more substantial was burning, or had recently burned, since the black smoke rose in thin tendrils rather than choking columns.

As a matter of habit, Fargo loosened his Colt in its holster. He was not concerned yet. There might be a perfectly logical explanation. But if living in the wild had taught him anything, it was that those who lived the longest were those who were wary of everything and everyone, and Fargo intended to live a good long while.

To his left a short way was the Platte River, as unspectacular a waterway as ever existed, fringed by greenery that depended on the river to thrive. To his right stretched the limitless prairie. Like the river, the prairie was depended on by a wealth of wildlife: buffalo, antelope, and deer, which in turn were food for roving wolves, coyotes, cougars, and bears.

Fargo rounded a bend and straightened in surprise.

The black tendrils rose from the charred skeleton of a cabin. A cabin that had not been there the last time Fargo passed this way. The stone chimney and a few large timbers were all that remained of the farmer's hopes and aspirations.

It brought a frown. A cabin suggested settlers, and settlers suggested a settlement, and there were already enough of those, in Fargo's opinion. More than enough. Each year thousands of emigrants flocked to the West. If it kept up, if the tide was not stemmed, eventually the West would be overrun and be no different from the East, where in some parts a man could not spit without hitting a neighbor.

Fargo would hate for that to happen. He liked his elbow room. He liked being free to roam the wild spaces as his whims moved him. Every new settlement took some of the wild space away. Every new settlement made him a little less free.

Fargo shut all that from his mind as he neared the homestead. A few acres of tilled soil and a small barn told him the owner of the cabin was a farmer. Or had been. He spotted bodies. Immediately he did two things; he drew rein and he yanked his Henry from the saddle scabbard. Levering a cartridge into the chamber, he studied the situation.

The bodies lay a dozen yards past what had been the rear of the cabin. Four corpses, laid out in a row from largest to smallest.

In front of the cabin, close enough to have been blackened by the fire but not so close as to burst into flame, sat a buckboard.

Fargo's first thought was that hostiles were to blame. The ill will between whites and the red men grew worse every year. The Indians naturally resented the white invasion, while the whites saw it as their divine right to claim for themselves land the Indians had roamed for untold generations.

The Sioux, the Arapaho, the Kiowa; warriors from any of the three might have paid the farm a visit.

Then Fargo saw tracks, and he knew hostiles were not to blame. The hoofprints had been made by shod mounts. Indian warhorses, as a rule, were not fitted with horseshoes. White men were responsible. Ten or more, Fargo judged.

Fargo's frown deepened. Outlaws and cutthroats were common on the frontier. All too common. The lawless flocked to where there was no law. To them, the West was an invite to kill, rob, and maim in an unending orgy of violence.

Gigging the Ovaro over to the bodies, Fargo felt anger take hold. Killing the farmer was one thing. Killing the farmer's wife another. Killing the children was the sort of vile atrocity only the worst of the badmen would do.

All four had been shot through the forehead. All four had been left with their hands folded across their chests. That last, and the placement of the bodies, struck Fargo as peculiar. Rabid killers rarely went to so much bother. But what was strangest of all, what sent a spark of worry shooting through him, were the red dots that speckled the pale figures.

Although loathe to leave the bodies unburied, Fargo

quickly reined past the cabin. If those red dots were what he thought they were, it explained the deaths and the burned cabin. The dots were also a warning to get the hell out of there.

Just then a shadow flitted across him. Glancing up, Fargo beheld several circling silhouettes. Wings outstretched, seeming to float, three vultures had gathered. Soon the sky would be thick with them.

Bending, Fargo slid his Henry into the saddle scabbard. Let the buzzards dispose of the dead. That was what buzzards did. In a few days there wouldn't be anything left. He glanced back at the bodies, and the distraction cost him.

Around the barn came two men. Shotguns were wedged to their shoulders. "Hold it right there, mister!"

Fargo reined up. He did not try for his Colt. Not with those hand howitzers trained on him. At that range there would not be enough of him left to scrape into a dustpan. "What's this?" he demanded.

"As if you don't know!" retorted the man on the left.

They were dressed the same, in overalls, boots, and homespun shirts. More farmers, by the looks of them.

"As last we've caught one of you murdering polecats!"

"I didn't kill those people," Fargo said.

"You expect us to believe that?" the man on the left rasped. He appeared to be the excitable type. "I ought to blow you in half for what you've done."

"Hold on, Glenn," the other man said. He had dark hair and a leaner build. "We shouldn't jump to conclusions."

"The hell you say, Russ," Glenn snapped. "How long before him and the rest of his pack pay us a visit? I don't know about you, but I damn well am not going to let them harm a hair on my sweet Glenda's head."

"I'm saying we shouldn't fly off the handle," Russ said.

Glenn bobbed his shotgun at the row of bodies. "You can say that with them lying yonder? Larry Sunman was our friend. We owe it to him and his loved ones to buck out this polecat in gore."

"Not without being sure," Russ said. "We saw this

fellow ride up. We saw how he reacted. Strikes me that maybe he's not a night rider."

Fargo took that as an opportunity to say, "I don't know what is going on here. I'm just passing through."

"Sure you are!" Glenn growled. Clearly, he yearned to squeeze the trigger.

The other farmer lowered his shotgun. "You can't hardly blame us for being on edge, mister. The Sunmans are the fourth family to be wiped out in the past month." He paused. "I'm Russ Cepna, by the way. My friend here is Glenn Handy. Who might you be?"

Fargo told them.

Russ Cepna's brow creased and he repeated, "Fargo? I've heard that name somewhere."

"So have I," Glenn Handy said. "But I can't rightly recollect where."

"I scout for the army," Fargo said by way of explanation. He did a lot of other things, too, but he figured that mentioning the military would make them a shade less apt to blow him into eternity.

"A scout, you say?" Russ's eyes widened. "Now I remember. I heard about you at Fort Kearney. You're the one who rescued that wagon train caught in the Sierras last winter. They ran out of food and started to eat one another. It was all anybody talked about for a while."

Glenn Handy, much to Fargo's relief, lowered his shotgun as well. But he was still suspicious. "Do you have any proof you are who you say you are?"

"You can come with me to Fort Kearney," Fargo suggested. "The commander knows me well."

Handy shook his head. "I'm not leaving my farm or my Glenda unprotected. If I do, the night riders will burn us out for sure."

"That's twice you've mentioned them," Fargo noted. "Who are they? What's it all about?"

Russ Cepna shuddered. The next word he uttered was voiced in a barely audible whisper. "Smallpox."

Fargo glanced toward the bodies. He was thinking of the red dots. His hunch had been right. Smallpox was held in utter dread. It struck without warning, and often nearly wiped out entire towns and settlements. The mere mention of the disease was enough to start a stampede of souls to healthier climes. "How bad is it?"

"Seven people have died of the pox so far," Russ said. "Over twenty if you count those the night riders have killed."

"What do they have to do with it?"

Glenn Handy answered, "They kill anyone who comes down with smallpox. Hell, they kill anyone they think *might* come down with it."

Fargo arched an eyebrow. Some communities would go to any lengths to halt the spread, but this was a new one on him. "Last I knew, that qualifies as murder, and murder is against the law."

"Wet Grass doesn't have a tin star," Russ revealed. "It's not big enough to need one."

"It could use a marshal now," Glenn said.

"Wet Grass?" Fargo never ceased to be amused at the names towns and settlements were given. Places like Little Hocking, Blue Balls, Titwell, and his favorite, Intercourse. He gestured at the ocean of grass to the south. There was plenty of it, sure, but it was the middle of the summer. "The prairie is as dry as tinder."

Russ explained, "There's a stretch farther on, close to the river, where the ground is a bit marshy and the grass is green all year long."

"Is there a saloon in this settlement of yours?" Fargo asked. It was too much to hope for. Most frontier communities were made up of Bible-fearing folk who regarded liquor as sinful.

"As a matter of fact, there is," Russ said. "The man who owns it now pretty much runs Wet Grass. He owns the general store, the stable, you name it. His name is Cole Narciss."

"It was him who sent us out here to check on the Sunmans," Glenn volunteered. "How about lending us a hand burying them?"

"Is that wise?" Fargo wondered. Smallpox was highly contagious. Those who came down with it were always quarantined. Fargo was unsure whether a dead person could give the disease to a live person, but he had no hankering to find out.

"Larry Sunman was our friend," Russ reiterated. "We have gloves and bandannas in our saddlebags. If we do it quick-like, we should be safe."

"We hope," Glenn amended.

"I don't have gloves," Fargo noted. "I'll help dig the graves but I won't touch the bodies."

"We're obliged for the help," Russ said. He disappeared around the corner and came back leading two horses.

The Ovaro nickered and shied, and Fargo didn't blame it.

One of the horses was a saddle horse, a sorrel as ordinary as rainwater. But the other was a monster. It had to be close to six feet at the shoulder and as broad as a grizzly. Massively built, it would tip the scales at somewhere close to fifteen hundred pounds. A striking shade of gray, it had a short mane and short legs.

"Is that a Percheron?" Fargo asked. In recent years Percherons were coming more into use as draft animals. They were fairly common east of the Mississippi, but much less so west of it.

"Sure is," Glenn said, taking the reins from Russ. "I brought it with me all the way from New Jersey. Paid a pretty penny for this beauty, I don't mind telling you." Beaming proudly, he reached up and patted the Percheron's neck. "It was my Glenda's idea. She likes big ones. She thought it would help make a success of our farm that much sooner."

Russ had leaned his shotgun against the barn and was taking heavy work gloves from his saddlebags. "Let's get this over with. I don't want to be near those bodies a minute longer than I have to."

Reluctantly, Fargo climbed down. "Did you bring a spare shovel?"

"We didn't think to bring any at all," Russ said. "But there should be tools in the barn."

The wide door was open part way. Fargo entered, then paused to let his eyes adjust. The stalls were empty. Bales of hay were stacked against the wall to his left. He did not see any tools, but there was a room at the back. The tools might be there. His spurs jingling, he moved down the center aisle. He hoped he was not making a mistake by sticking around to help. Smallpox was not to be taken lightly. He was almost to the room when an apparition shuffled out of the gloom toward him.

It was a man. A spindly spider of a man in shabby clothes and a well-worn brown vest, his pale skull of a face sprinkled with red splotches. His mouth opened and closed but no sounds came out.

"Hold it!" Fargo warned.

The apparition extended a gnarled hand and reached for him.

2

It was rare for Skye Fargo's skin to crawl, but it crawled now. He flung himself back. In pure reflex his right hand swooped to his Colt, but he did not draw. The man was sick, deathly ill with smallpox, and too far gone to realize the danger he posed to others. "Stop!" Fargo barked.

The man did no such thing. Groaning hideously, his eyelids fluttering, he extended his other arm and continued to shamble forward.

Backpedaling, Fargo evaded a clawing hand. He dodged right, then left. Passing a stall, his arm brushed a broom. Instantly, Fargo snatched it up and thrust it at the spindly horror's chest. "Stand still, damn it."

The man stopped and stared blankly at the bristles. He voiced an inarticulate cry and knocked the broom aside with a sweep of a thin arm.

Fargo was almost caught flat-footed. The man's dirty fingernails missed his face by inches. Retreating, he used the broom to keep the man from reaching him. "If you don't stop, I'll shoot you in the leg," he warned. "So help me." He did not want to, but he could not let the man touch him.

A ghastly groan rose to the rafters. The man focused on Fargo with inhuman intensity.

Fargo had meant what he said. The Colt leaped into his hand, but before he could shoot the speckled apparition sprang with surprising speed. Barely in time, Fargo skipped aside. He found himself with his back to a stall, and the way out cut off.

The man's waxen features contorted, but whether in a grimace or a grin, Fargo couldn't say.

Suddenly light flooded the barn. Russ Cepna had opened the door all the way and was saying, "What's taking so long—" Catching sight of the man, he blurted, "Byerly! What in God's name?"

The living nightmare turned toward the farmer. Curling his fingers like talons, Byerly lurched toward him.

"Byerly, no!" Russ skipped backward, or tried to. He tripped and fell to one knee.

The thing called Byerly was almost on him when a shotgun blasted. In the confines of the barn it sounded as if a cannon had gone off. The effect of the buckshot was about the same as a cannonball. Byerly's head imitated an overripe pumpkin bursting. From his chin up, all that was left of him was a few flaps of skin and scalp, and his jawbone.

Deprived of whatever life force had animated the bundle of bones, the man collapsed.

"Sorry I had to do that," Glenn Handy said. "He should have known not to try and touch any of us."

"You knew him?" Fargo asked.

Russ Cepna nodded as he slowly rose. "He was a hired hand who worked for Larry Sunman in exchange for meals and a place to sleep."

"A nice enough cuss," Glenn Handy said by way of an epitaph. "The smallpox must have affected his mind."

Fargo had never heard that mentioned as one of the symptoms, but it was as good an explanation as any of the man's behavior. He started to walk past the prone ruin, and abruptly stopped. Byerly's brown vest was open, and there, low down near the belt, was a blood-rimmed hole in Byerly's shirt.

Russ noticed, too. "That's quite a spread for buckshot."

Fargo was skeptical. Buckshot was made up of lead balls that spread out with distance, so that the spread was greater at thirty feet than at ten. But Byerly had been less than six feet from Glenn Handy when the farmer fired. The shot would not have spread that much. He bent closer, but not too close, and discovered that the

10

hole was actually a vertical slit. "This man has been stabbed."

"What?" both Russ and Glenn said at the same time. They began to bend down, then glanced at one another and hastily stepped back.

"How in heaven's name can that be?" Russ Handy asked neither of them in particular. "Unless"—and he snapped his fingers—"the night riders were to blame. They thought they had killed him but they were wrong."

"If that's so," Russ said, "why didn't they lay him outside with the Sunman family?"

"How would I know?" Glenn said. "Maybe he got away from them and hid, so they went off and left him."

"All this guessing won't get the burying done any sooner," Russ said. He turned to Fargo. "What about those shovels?"

The back room contained plenty of tools. Fargo handed shovels to the farmers and selected a pick for himself. To do it right they had to dig down deep so scavengers could not get at the remains. The better part of the morning passed as they dug a large enough hole for all the Sunmans and a smaller grave for Byerly. At last they wearily straightened and stepped back.

"That should do it," Russ said. "Any scavenger that digs down that far is welcome to stuff itself."

Fargo figured the farmers would simply roll the bodies into the holes, but they would not hear of it.

"They were our friends," Russ said. "They deserve to be planted decently."

"We should have brought blankets," Glenn remarked. "But I didn't think to bring any."

"Me neither," Russ said. "If I had known in advance they had come down with the pox, I would have."

"I thought you said someone sent you out here?" Fargo reminded him. "Didn't he know?"

"Narciss sent us to check, sure," Glenn responded. "Because Larry and his family hadn't been seen in Wet Grass in a spell. But that wasn't unusual. Larry and his family kept to themselves. He liked it out here. Liked the flat and the emptiness."

"What do we wrap them with?" Russ got back to the matter at hand.

The pair stared at the Ovaro, and the bedroll tied to the saddle.

Fargo did not want to part with any of his blankets, but neither did he care to stand there arguing about it until the cows came home. He shoved them at Russ. "Do what you have to."

The two farmers tied bandannas over the lower half of their faces, slipped on heavy gloves, and spread out the blankets. Since there were only two, they placed the father and mother on one, and the son and daughter on the other. After wrapping the blankets as tight as they could, they coiled rope around the grisly bundles so there was no chance the bodies would slip out. Then, with extreme care, they lowered the family into the grave.

"God have mercy," Glenn breathed as he stepped back. "I'd rather be doing anything other than planting these poor folks."

"Be thankful it's not us being planted," Russ said.

Byerly was not treated with the same dignity. The farmers used the broom and a pitchfork to roll the body from the barn to the grave, and dumped him in.

Filling in the graves took the better part of twenty minutes. They had finished and were tamping down the dirt when hooves drummed to the east.

"I wonder who that can be?" Glenn said.

The answer came in the form of five riders who swept past the barn and came to a stop in a swirl of dust. The five were cast in the same coarse mold; their features were cold, their bearing unfriendly, the grips of the revolvers on their hips well worn. The foremost was taller and broader than the rest, and had the added distinction of a thick mustache with curled ends and a small beard that barely covered his chin and came to a point. He also wore a costlier set of store-bought clothes and a hat with a wider brim.

"Cole Narciss's men," Russ mentioned.

Almost casually, the lead rider moved his jacket aside,

revealing a pearl-handled Remington. His dark eyes fixed on the fresh mounds of dirt. "What in hell are those?"

"What does it look like, Pyle?" Glenn replied. "Graves. You're just in time to help us say a few words over the dear departed."

"I can see they are graves," Pyle said testily. "I can also see the cabin has burned down. The night riders have been here."

"Either that, or someone was mighty careless with a lamp," Glenn said.

Pyle did not appreciate the sarcasm. "If the night riders paid them a visit, that means Sunman and his family had smallpox."

"Why else would we have buried them?" was Glenn's response.

To Fargo, it was plain the two did not like each other. It was also plain the farmer was playing with leaden fire. Pyle had the look of someone who liked to use his six-gun to settle disputes.

Russ Cepna tried playing peacemaker. "It's all been taken care of, Kutyer. Everything is fine."

"Not if you touched them, it isn't," Pyle Kutyer said. "You know Mr. Narciss's rules."

"We used the gloves we're wearing," Russ said. "We were careful."

"You've been exposed." Kutyer made it sound like they were doomed. "You know what that means. You will have to be quarantined."

"Like hell," Glenn said. "We don't have any of the symptoms and we're damn sure not going."

"I'm not asking you, I'm telling you," Pyle said. "That goes for you too, stranger," he said, finally acknowledging Fargo's presence.

Fargo looked at Russ, who wore a worried expression. "Quarantined?"

"Thrown in a pen about a mile south of Wet Grass. It was Cole Narciss's idea. Anyone who is exposed to smallpox is kept there until Narciss is sure they aren't coming down with it."

"No one is putting me in any pen," Fargo informed them.

Pyle Kutyer disagreed. "We'll put you any damn place we please. It's not just your hide at stake. It's the whole settlement." He nodded at the men with him and they kneed their mounts, spreading in a half circle. "Shed that hogleg of yours."

Fargo understood why Glenn Handy did not like Kutyer. He had taken a dislike to him, too. "Go to hell."

A squat toad on Pyle Kutyer's left stiffened. "Mister, folks calls me Greasy Joe. I've blown out the wicks of seven men so far, and I will sure as hell blow out yours if you don't do exactly as Pyle tells you to. Unbuckle that gun belt and let it drop."

"Not today, not ever," Fargo said. While he appreciated their desire to protect the settlement, their highhanded attitude rankled. And he would be damned if he would let them coop him up in some pen for God knew how long.

Greasy Joe's dark eyes glittered. "Can I take this one, Pyle? He's begging for it, and I'm itching to give it to him."

"Be my guest," Pyle Kutyer said.

Greasy Joe licked his thick toad lips as if he were about to bite into a juicy bug. "I should thank you, stranger. I do so love to shoot folks."

Fargo did not say anything. He was watching the others. Apparently they were content to let Greasy Joe handle him. Their mistake.

"The last gent I bucked out in gore," Greasy Joe bragged, "never cleared leather. I'm about as fast as they come."

"As ugly as they come, too."

"What do you suppose your brains will look like outside your head?" Greasy Joe taunted.

"I have a question first," Fargo said.

"Oh?" Greasy Joe smirked. "This should be interesting. What might it be?"

"Who buries you, after? Because it sure as hell won't be me."

14

Greasy Joe's toad face flushed. "You smug bastard. In about three seconds you'll be burning in hell." He started his draw.

Fargo's hand was a blur. His Colt was out and spat lead and smoke before Greasy Joe's revolver rose an inch. The slug slapped the center of Greasy Joe's forehead with a loud *thwack* and Greasy Joe flung out his arms and pitched from his saddle.

The others were frozen in shock until one of Greasy Joe's companions blurted, "Lordy! Did you see that?"

"I saw," Pyle Kutyer said. His eyebrows were pinched together, and he was studying Fargo with a mix of puzzlement and respect. "I'm impressed, mister, and it takes a lot to impress me. Mind telling me your handle?"

"I've plumb forgot," Fargo said. He wagged the Colt. "Suppose you and your friends light a shuck. Take the tub of lard with you. We don't want to give the buzzards bellyaches."

"I never argue with the muzzle of a gun," Pyle said. He flicked a finger at two of the riders. They climbed down and proceeded to hoist Greasy Joe over his saddle. A lot of straining and grunting was involved but they got it done, using Joe's rope to tie him on, then climbed back on their mounts.

Pyle had a parting comment for the two farmers. "You've been spared the pen for now. But this isn't over. As soon as we get back, I'm going straight to Cole. He's not likely to let it rest."

"You tell him we'll stay at our farms until we're sure one way or the other," Russ said. "That should satisfy him."

Glenn stabbed a finger at Kutyer. "Tell him, too, that neither him nor you nor any of these curly wolves are to set foot on our property."

"Was that a threat, Handy?" Pyle Kutyer asked.

"Call it whatever you want," Glenn said. "Just so you get it through your thick skulls that if you come anywhere near my Glenda and me, there will be hell to pay."

"I'll pass on the word to Mr. Narciss." Pyle glanced at Fargo, touched his hat brim, and wheeled his bay.

The quartet departed in a flurry of dust. Fargo did not slide the Colt into his holster until they were well out of rifle range.

"This is bad," Russ said. "This is very bad."

"How do you figure?" Glenn responded. "We sent them skulking off with their tails between their legs, didn't we?"

"He did," Russ said, with a jerk of his thumb at Fargo. "But you know Cole Narciss as well as I do. Pyle was right. Cole will want to punish us." He looked at Fargo. "As for you, friend, I shudder to think what he will do to you."

3

Skye Fargo was amazed at how fast settlements and towns sprang up. Gold was found in a high-country stream, and within weeks buildings sprouted like clover. A tavern was built at a crossroads and before long it was the hub of scores of homes. The army established a fort somewhere, and in no time the countryside around it was crammed with settlers who liked the idea of living close to its protective walls.

Here, deep in the heart of Nebraska Territory, was another example. Wet Grass had not existed the last time Fargo rode through, but now a score of buildings lined a street. The town was not on the Oregon Trail but a stone's throw north of it, and close to the Platte River.

Most of the houses were simple frame affairs, except for one that stood apart from the rest and was three times as big. There was the inevitable stable, a general store and a feed and grain combined, and the establishment Fargo was eager to visit, the saloon. No horses were at the hitch rail, he noticed. The saloon itself was as quiet as a church on any day of the week except Sunday. Since it was the middle of the afternoon, that wasn't unusual.

Fargo strolled in with his thumbs hooked in his belt. The sawdust on the floor, the spittoons, the poker tables, the familiar odors of stale cigar smoke and liquor, stirred memories of other saloons and of sultry pleasures.

The bartender had a great gray beard that hung down to his waist and a friendly twinkle in his eyes. A red streak Fargo could not account for ran down the center of the beard. At the moment he was cleaning glasses in a bucket of water, which was rather remarkable. Bartenders in frontier saloons were rarely so conscientious; a swipe of a dirty rag, and a glass was clean enough to get by.

"What will your poison be, mister?"

"Whiskey. A bottle of your best." Fargo asked how much and plunked coins on the bar.

The bartender opened the bottle and set it and a glass in front of him. "I'm Jim Fina. My wife Jackie is in the back. She can rustle up some grub if you're hungry."

"Pleased to meet you." Fargo indulged in a good, long swig. The red-eye burned clear down to his stomach. He smacked his lips, relishing the taste, and asked, "Do you own this place?"

"Would that I did. I run it for someone else. His name is Cole Narciss. He pretty much runs things hereabouts."

Fargo recollected one of the farmers mentioning the name. "I heard somewhere that he pretty much runs the settlement."

"If by run you mean owns most of it," Jim Fina said. "The store, the stable, and half the houses in town, all belong to Narciss. He rents out the houses. His own is that big one at the end of the street."

Fargo motioned at the empty room. "Sort of dead around here during the day, isn't it?"

"It used to be a livelier," Jim Fina said. "But folks are scared to come out much thanks to the epidemic." He paused meaningfully. "Smallpox. Which is why you might want to take that bottle and fan the breeze."

"Have a lot of people left?" Fargo asked, thinking that might account for the empty street.

"Oh, no," Fina said. "Many would like to. There's nothing like smallpox to make a body wonder what the inside of a coffin looks like. But they can't."

"What's stopping them?"

The voice that answered came from the front of the saloon. It was a voice that made Fargo think of the grinding a wagon axle made when the axle grease dried up, or the sound of a blacksmith's hammer scraping an anvil. "I am," the voice said. "No one leaves Wet Grass without my say-so."

Fargo saw the bartender take a step back. He slowly turned, the bottle in his left hand, his right hand close to his Colt.

Two men had entered. One was Pyle Kutyer. Kutyer stood behind and to one side of the other.

"That's Cole Narciss," Jim Fina whispered.

Fargo had guessed as much. He did not know what kind of man he was expecting Narciss to be, but it certainly did not match the reality.

Wet Grass's leading citizen had a melon of a head perched on a washtub of a body. An expensive suit, a derby, and polished boots lent a splash of money to his appearance. His moon face was uncommonly pale, suggesting he spent most of his time indoors. From under the derby spilled bushy sideburns that flared to points. He came toward the bar, moving with an odd, waddling gait that brought to mind the waddle of an overfed goose.

Jim Fina quickly produced a bottle of rye and two glasses. "Is there anything else I can get for you, Mr. Narciss?"

"If there is I will let you know," the washtub said with an air of self-importance.

He stood and waited while Pyle Kutyer poured drinks for both of them and slid a glass to his waiting hand. "You know who I am." It was a statement, not a question, and he said it without looking at Fargo.

"God Almighty."

"Scoff if you want, but in these parts that is damn close to the truth. I'm Cole Narciss, and I own this settlement lock, stock, and barrel." Narciss raised the glass to his thick lips and took a delicate sip. He gave the impression that he did not enjoy the rye but was only drinking it for appearance's sake.

Fargo stood so he was facing them. Narciss did not

appear to have a sidearm but Pyle Kutyer had that pearl-handled Remington, and men who wore revolvers with fancy handles seldom did so for bluff or ballast.

"You killed a man who worked for me today," Cole Narciss said as casually as if they were discussing the weather.

"He shouldn't have tried to kill me."

"He was acting under my orders for the greater good of the community. By refusing to cooperate, you put everyone else at risk."

Fargo was in no mood to be lectured. "Was he wearing a badge?"

The question seemed to confound Narciss. "Well, no, but—"

"Are you the law?"

"No, I am not, but see here—"

Fargo did not let Narciss finish. "Then he had no right to tell me what to do, and you had no right telling him to throw his weight around."

Pyle Kutyer had been leaning against the bar, but now he stepped away from it with his arms at his sides. "Show more respect. Mr. Narciss doesn't have to explain himself to every drifter who comes along."

"You must have me confused with someone who gives a damn."

Kutyer moved his jacket aside, exposing the pearl handles. "Maybe we should settle this here and now."

To Fargo's mild surprise, Cole Narciss intervened. "Enough of that, Pyle, if you please. Our visitor has a point. Perhaps I did overstep my bounds." He set his drink down and spread his pudgy hands. "What do you say we start over again? This time on the right foot?" Narciss offered his hand. "You know who I am but I have no idea who you are. Would you mind remedying that?"

Fargo obliged.

For the fleetest instant, Cole Narciss seemed to freeze. But then the instant passed, and he shook warmly and said, "I trust there are no hard feelings? I will be sure my men are more careful in the future."

"They'll go on breathing longer if they are." Fargo

chugged more whiskey. He figured that was the end of it but Narciss had more on his mind.

"Are you, by any chance, planning to move on?"

"I don't intend to spend the rest of my life in this fly speck," Fargo admitted.

"Might I ask where you are bound?"

Fargo saw no harm in telling him. "St. Louis."

"In that case, perhaps you will hear me out," Narciss requested. "You know about the smallpox: and I trust you are aware of how deadly it can be. One person can infect an entire city. Imagine the consequences if, say, you were to ride on to St. Louis and then come down with the disease."

The whiskey turned sour in Fargo's mouth.

"I don't need to stress, do I, that you would be accountable for everyone who was afflicted? Do you want that on your conscience? I know I wouldn't."

Fargo hated to admit it, but the overfed dandy had a point. He recalled the time he had passed through an Indian village decimated by smallpox: the bodies everywhere, the women and children who had died in the most awful agony. "No, I would not want that."

"Then perhaps you are open to a suggestion?" Cole Narciss asked in his suave manner. "Stick around a while. If you haven't contracted the smallpox in, say, seven to ten days, then it is probably safe for you to go on your way. Doesn't that seem sensible?"

The notion of being stuck in Wet Grass for that long held as much appeal to Fargo as having a tooth pulled, but he conceded. "Sensible enough."

A grin split Narciss from ear to ear. "Good. And don't look so glum. Wet Grass is not without its charms. You will see for yourself soon enough, I would imagine." He took another reluctant sip of the rye, set it down with an exaggerated sigh, and announced, "I am afraid business calls me away. But I would very much like to talk with you later, if you are willing."

"I'll be right here," Fargo said.

"I was hoping you would come to my house. Say, about ten?"

"Kind of late for a social call," Fargo remarked.

"Not for me," Cole Narciss assured him. "I stay up to all hours of the night. Ten o'clock is early." With Pyle Kutyer dogging his heels, the lord and master of Wet Grass departed.

Jim Fina mopped his perspiring brow with his sleeve. "Dang, that was something! I never saw anyone stand up to him like you just done. It's a miracle he didn't have Kutyer turn you into a sieve."

"Didn't you mention something about food?"

"Sure did. My missus, Jackie, is the best cook this side of creation. Want me to fetch her to take your order?"

"I'll be at the corner table," Fargo said with a nod. It gave him a clear view of the entire saloon, and had the added advantage that no one could get at him from behind. Propping his boots up, he deliberately gouged his spurs into the table. He was on his third chug when a lively eyed gal came out of the back wiping her hands on her apron.

"I'm Jackie Fina. My husband says you would like a bite to eat." She noticed his boots. "You're liable to scratch the table something awful sitting like that."

"It's Narciss's table, isn't it?"

Jackie blinked, then grinned and glanced at the front door. "Far be it for me to spoil your fun. Scratch all you want."

"I take it you don't think much of him?" Fargo had a lot of information to unearth and he might as well get started.

"I don't like to speak ill of folks," the bartender's wife said, "but I could not think any less of Cole Narciss if I tried. He is a pompous ass." Catching herself, she covered her mouth, then said, "Forgive my strong language. I tend to forget that a lady should not say certain things."

"What can you tell me about him?" Fargo inquired. "How long has he been here? How many hardcases does he have riding for him? How long ago did the epidemic start? Has anyone sent for a sawbones?"

"Mercy me!" Jackie laughed nervously and gave the

front door another wary glance. "I wouldn't mind answering all those. Really I wouldn't. But Jim and me like it here. If Mr. Narciss found out I talked to you, he would have one of his riders drag me by a rope."

"No one would do that to a woman," Fargo said. On the frontier, the female gender was as highly regarded as gold. Anyone who harmed a woman became the guest of honor at a hemp social.

Jackie Fina shrugged. "Think what you will. But Cole Narciss isn't like most men. He is twisted inside. He likes to grind his boot heels on those who rile him, and he doesn't care if it's male or female."

Fargo wanted to press her for more information but thought better of it. "In that case, bring me a steak smothered in onions, a loaf of bread and butter, and whatever else suits your fancy."

Jackie hustled off, and Fargo sat back and chugged more whiskey. A lot of pondering was called for. He never liked to see anyone ride roughshod over others. But it was not as if the people in Wet Grass were being forced to live there. As soon as the epidemic ran its course, they could pull up stakes for wherever they wanted. Besides, he couldn't go around butting his nose in where it didn't belong or pretty soon it would be shot off.

Along about then the front door opened and in sashayed three bundles of loveliness. Fargo froze with the bottle halfway to his mouth, marveling at the last sight he had ever figured to behold in a place like Wet Grass.

In the lead was a buxom blonde in a red dress so tight it was a wonder she could inhale without popping every button. She had blues eyes and full red lips, and a vixenish strut that advertised she knew she was easy on the eyes.

After her came a bubbly wench with a fondness for pink: pink hair, pink lips, pink fingernails, and a pink dress that, while not as tight as the blonde's, left no doubt as to her playful nature.

Third was a redhead with a shape an hourglass would

envy, a blue dress that appeared to have been painted on, and a pouty mouth that invited any man who saw it to smother it with his own.

The three visions were as dumbfounded by Fargo as he was by them. Sauntering over, they regarded him much as a pack of she-wolves might regard a den mate.

"My oh my," cooed the voluptuous blonde. "What do we have here?"

"I think I've died and gone to heaven," the pink morsel declared.

"Now, now, girls," purred the redhead. "He's a big 'un. There's more than enough to go around. What say we draw straws to see who gets to rip those buckskins off first?"

4

Fargo stared at the whiskey bottle. "I can't be seeing things. I haven't had enough yet."

Laughing, the blonde leaned over the table to display her wares. "Has anyone ever mentioned you are a handsome cuss?"

"It's the beard," said the woman in pink. "I always have liked the hairy ones. Especially when they lisp."

"I like them manly," the redhead remarked. "But before we get ahead of ourselves, maybe I should introduce us."

The blonde, it turned out, was Cat Sultraine. Appropriately enough, the woman in pink called herself Pinky Belle. The redhead was Jasmine Keller. They sat at his table and stared so hungrily at Fargo that he was willing to bet they would soon start drooling.

"You ladies act as if you are half starved for men."

"Not half, honey-chile," Pinky said. "Fully starved. There hasn't been a wagon train stop at Wet Grass since the smallpox began."

"And the locals don't count," Cat Sultraine said. "Their wives would shoot us dead if we so much as touched one."

"There were five of us until a short while ago," Jasmine commented. "But Helen Duckers went and married a local, Steve Sherwood, and Kim Midge took off to Arkansas or some such place to be with kin."

"If it's so slow," Fargo asked, "why don't you pack

up and find someplace livelier, like Kansas City or New Orleans?"

"You're forgetting the smallpox," Cat said.

"We can't leave until the epidemic is over," Pinky revealed.

"It's too dangerous," Jasmine elaborated. "None of us have any of the symptoms, but Mr. Narciss has convinced us we shouldn't put others at risk."

"He made the same case with me."

"Mr. Narciss can be hard at times," Jasmine mentioned, "but he's only doing what he thinks is best for the settlement."

"That's right," Cat Sultraine agreed. "He's a post when it comes to bending to accommodate folks, but this time we agree with him."

"We just wish the epidemic was over with," Pinky said. "If we were any more bored, we would count our nose hairs for fun."

Fargo nearly snorted whiskey out his nose. "I'm glad it hasn't come to that," he said with a grin. "How about if I treat you to some red-eye and we get better acquainted?"

They were more than willing. Fargo barely got a word in as they chatted up three storms. He learned they had been hired in St. Louis by Cole Narciss, who had promised them they would make more money in Wet Grass.

"That was true until the epidemic," Cat said. "Regular as clockwork, wagon trains came through."

"A lot of them were starved for female company," Pinky observed. "But then, men will always be men."

"Personally," Jasmine said, with a mischievous twinkle in her green eyes, "I like it that way."

More small talk followed. Fargo dampened their feisty spirits when he fished for information by asking, "What can you ladies tell me about the night riders I've heard about?"

"Where did you hear about them?" Jasmine asked.

Fargo told them about the Sunman farm. They grew downcast at the news. Cat Sultraine drained half her glass at a gulp and sadly shook her head.

"That's too bad. Larry was as nice as they come. He

had this cat he'd tote around. A stray he picked up some-where. His wife used to say he loved that cat more than he loved her."

"Byerly is dead too, you say?" Pinky said. "That's a shame. He was one of the few single men hereabouts. I always thought he was a bit touched in the head, the way he went on about some critter he claimed he saw once down in Texas. Something called a three-toed skunk ape."

"What upsets me the most," Jasmine said, "is that poor Larry and Byerly won't be the last. There's no tell-ing who will come down with the damn disease next."

"About those night riders," Fargo prompted.

"Oh. Them," Jasmine said. "There's not much we can tell you. They wear hoods and they go around at night killing folks who have the disease. So it won't spread to their own families, most likely."

"Then the night riders are settlers?"

"They could be anyone," Cat said. "But whoever they are, they have no right to do what they are doing."

"Some of the farmers have had enough," Jasmine dis-closed. "They want to go to the army for help, but Nar-ciss won't hear of it. He says they might spread the smallpox to the soldiers."

"Aren't you ladies afraid of catching it?"

"Of course," Cat replied. "When we're not at work we stay in our rooms. Used to be I hardly spent any time there."

"I am so tired of staring at four walls I could scream," Pinky said. "I'm bound for New Orleans as soon as we can leave. They have opera there. And the most fra-grant soaps."

Jasmine reached across the table and laid her hand on Fargo's arm. Her skin was warm against his. "It's just your luck to be in the wrong place at the wrong time. I hope you will make the best of it."

Fargo did not have to ask what she meant. Along about then his food came. He heartily began eating, then noticed that the three lovelies looked longingly at his heaped plate. He ordered food for them, too.

Pretty soon a knee rubbed his right leg. Then a different knee rubbed his left. Somehow, yet a third knee got between his legs and stroked back and forth. Once, Cat and Pinky gave a start and glanced at one another, and he figured they had accidentally rubbed their own knees. He smothered a laugh.

The food and more small talk carried them until sunset. That was when customers strayed in, men from the settlement, done with their work for the day and wanting to relax before they headed home.

Shortly after, a strapping farmer entered and the other patrons fell silent. He came straight for Fargo's table and doffed his cap. "How do you do, my fine flowers?"

"This is John Busby, an immigrant from England," Cat told Fargo. "He's one of the few farmers who still comes in for a bottle now and then."

"Just don't tell the other half," Busby said, "or I'll be in the doghouse again."

"You spend so much time there," Pinky teased, "it's a wonder you don't go around with a collar."

"Every married man is on a leash, love," John Busby said. "You just can't see the leashes because they are invisible."

"Be careful, John," Jasmine said, nodding at men at the bar. "Not everyone is happy to see you. They are worried you'll bring the smallpox down on them and their families."

"Bloody nonsense," Busby said. "Neither me nor mine have the symptoms. Besides, Steve wants me to fetch a bottle for him and Helen. They're celebrating. They just found out she is in the family way."

It was Fargo who first became aware of the three stern-faced men in store-bought clothes who were drifting from the bar toward their table. He shifted so he had access to his revolver and remarked, "Friends of yours?"

Busby turned. Clenching his fist, he growled, "If those blokes are looking for trouble, they'll get it."

"Don't you dare, John," Jasmine cautioned. "You know Mr. Narciss doesn't permit fighting in here."

Fargo decided to do the farmer a favor. He stood up, stared hard at the three men, and placed his hand on his

Colt. As one, they came to a stop. After a few whispered words, they wheeled and returned to the bar. Fargo sat back down.

"Did you see that!" John Busby declared. "I scared those blighters off." Chuckling, he turned back to the table. "But I better not push my luck. I'll buy the bottles and head on home."

As the farmer walked off, Jasmine let out a sigh. "You can see how it is," she said to Fargo. "The suspicion. The hate. It grows worse every day."

"If it keeps up," Cat said, "farmers won't be able to come into Wet Grass without being shot at."

"I wish people could get along," Pinky said. "This world would be a better place to live."

Fargo barely heard her. Under the table, a hand was slowly rubbing inward from his knee. This time there was no mistaking which of them was the naughty culprit. Jasmine was bent half sideways, her other elbow on the table, looking as innocent as innocent could be.

"I do so hope you don't have any plans for later, handsome."

"As a matter of fact, I do," Fargo said, and was amused by her severe disappointment. "Cole Narciss asked me to stop by his place at ten o'clock tonight." Not that he really wanted to.

The women were suddenly interested.

"What does he want to see you about?" Cat inquired.

"Hardly anyone ever gets to visit his house," Pinky revealed. "No one I know, other than Pyle Kutyer, has ever been inside."

"I wouldn't go if he begged me," Jasmine said. "There's something about him that gives me butterflies."

Fargo admired how she could caress his leg and carry on a casual conversation without batting a lovely eyelash. Taking his hand off his Colt, he slid his fingers onto her leg and slowly rubbed in small circles along her inner thigh. She stiffened slightly at the contact, then a pleased smile curled her full lips.

"What are you so happy about?" Cat Sultraine asked.

"Just a mood I'm in, I guess," Jasmine answered sweetly.

Pinky rose and smoothed her dress. "I suppose we should get to work, girls, and do what Mr. Narciss is paying us to do."

More men from the settlement had drifted in. The bar was lined end to end and card games were underway.

"Do we have to?" Cat pouted. "Fargo, here, is a heap more fun than any of those frumps."

"You wouldn't want Mr. Narciss to catch us frittering our time away, would you?" Pinky rejoined. "Remember when he caught me playing solitaire that time? He about broke my wrist, he twisted it so hard."

Still pouting, Cat Sultraine rose and trailed after Pinky Belle. Jasmine Keller started to follow them, then skipped in close to Fargo and whispered, "How about tonight at my place? After you're done with Narciss?"

"I don't know what time it will be," Fargo said.

"I don't get off until midnight," Jasmine whispered. "If you're done before that, you can walk me home. If it's after, I have a room in the third house down on the right, the bottom floor, at the very back." Smiling seductively, she, too, smoothed her dress, but only where it covered her thighs. "What do you say?"

Fargo felt twitching where he had not felt twitching in a while. "Wild horses couldn't keep me away."

After that the minutes crawled. Fargo went over to sit in on a poker game, but changed his mind when he discovered they were playing with toothpicks instead of money or chips. Bottle in hand, he strayed outdoors.

A multitude of stars had blossomed, and a quarter moon cast a wan, silvery glow. Wet Grass lay quiet under the mantle of night. Here and there, lamplight shone in windows. In the big house at the end of the street nearly every window was ablaze.

It was only a little past nine. Since Fargo had time to spare, he untied the Ovaro from the hitch rail and led the pinto down to the stable. There were plenty of empty stalls. He paid for the use of one for the night, and left his saddle and saddlebags in the tack room. With the Henry in the crook of his left arm, he made for the other end of the street, and the big house. It was shy of ten but he figured the sooner he went, the sooner he could get it over with, and the sooner he could be with Jasmine. He was looking forward to that. Jasmine had the sort of shapely, alluring body men hankered after.

A white picket fence surrounded the big house. The gate was closed. Fargo was about to swing it open when a faint sound from the rear of the house perked his curiosity. A horse had whinnied and been immediately silenced, as if by a hand over its muzzle.

Fargo took his time. He was not worried about being spotted. The light from the windows did not reach the fence.

A few trees grew close by, cottonwoods mostly. He threaded in among them and was almost to the last one when movement compelled him to drop to one knee.

Figures were moving about, half a dozen or more. Others waited on horseback. What they were up to was impossible to tell. The windows at the back were dark, the figures shrouded in murk.

Fargo wanted a closer look. Easing onto his belly, he crawled along the bottom of the fence. He was almost to the corner when the back door opened. Out strode a tall man. There was something odd about his head, and it was a few moments before Fargo realized the man who had just emerged, and everyone else, wore a hood.

"Was he in there?" a man on horseback asked.

"I couldn't find any sign of him," the tall man responded. "I don't know where he could have gotten to."

"We can't wait here all night," another shadowy figure complained. "Someone might spot us."

"Few are out this late," the tall man said. "Fewer still come anywhere near this house."

Fargo came to the corner. He had been holding the Henry against his side. Now he slid it forward so he could grip it with both hands. Inadvertently, the stock struck one of the fence slats.

The men at the back of the house swung in his direction. "What was that?" one wondered aloud.

The next moment a hooded rider kneed his mount toward Fargo.

5

Fargo froze. Flat on the ground, shrouded in shadow, he was confident the rider would not spot him. At any moment he expected the rider to rein around. But the man kept coming, growing closer and closer until the horse was almost to the corner of the fence.

The rider drew rein. His hood, with holes cut for the eyes and a slit for the mouth, swung from side to side. He lifted the reins to go back.

For a few moments Fargo thought he was safe.

Then the man's chin dipped. A harsh bellow rent the night air. "What the hell! There's somebody over here!" Even as he yelled, the man clawed at a pistol.

Fargo could not jump up and run. They would see him and bring him down before he went ten feet.

The man's revolver swept up and out. Fargo rolled onto his back as a dirt geyser erupted next to his head. He fired from the hip.

An invisible mallet snapped the rider's head back. His arm rose to the sky as if in appeal, and he tumbled.

From over a dozen throats rose yells and oaths. Several hooded riders spurred their animals toward the corner of the fence, firing as they came.

Fargo scrambled back and hugged the dank soil. It did no good. They had a fair idea where he was and they were firing as fast as they could work the hammers of their revolvers and rifles. Slugs tore through slats and sent wood slivers flying. Others peppered the ground.

Surging onto a knee, Fargo banged off a shot. One of the riders cried out and clutched at a shoulder.

Fargo could not drop them all. There were too many. But he received a reprieve from an unlikely source. The tall man by the back door roared, "Enough! The settlers will hear! Light a shuck, *now*!"

Just like that, to Fargo's amazement, the whole passel galloped off into the night, the man who had been wounded helped by another. Within seconds the dark had swallowed them. Their pounding hoofbeats faded.

By then many of the inhabitants of Wet Grass had ventured from their frame houses or from the saloon and were converging on the big house at the end of the street. Some had the forethought to bring lanterns. On arriving at the gate a general hubbub ensued.

"What was all that shooting about?"

"Anyone see anything?"

"Do you suppose someone shot Cole Narciss?"

"Wait! Who's that yonder? Toward the back, there!"

Fargo was standing over the disjointed heap he had blasted from the saddle. The settlers flowed toward him in a great wave, a wave that broke and came to stop when the glow of their lanterns revealed the hooded figure. A stunned silence descended with the abruptness of an avalanche, but it did not last.

"Look!" an elderly woman breathed. "It's one of the night riders!"

"Who is the hombre who shot him? Anyone know?"

"He just showed up today. I saw him at the saloon earlier."

"His name is Fargo."

That last sounded like Jim Fina.

Hunkering, Fargo tugged on the hood. It was made of burlap, and it would not come off. Binder twine had been tied around the bottom to hold it in place. Fargo pried with a fingernail and the knot came undone. He gave another tug and the burlap bag slid up over the man's face.

The settlers crowded close, forming a circle around the body, those in the back pushing against those in front.

"Anyone know him?" Fargo asked.

A stocky individual shook his head. "Never saw him before, mister."

"It's sure not a farmer," a skinny man commented. "I know every plow-pusher by sight."

"And he's not from Wet Grass, either," said someone else.

"But I thought the night riders were supposed to be locals," yet another man brought up.

Based on the ripple of excited conversation that followed, he was not the only one who was confused.

Fargo went through the night rider's pockets. He found a handful of coins and a folding knife. The man's horse had not strayed far, and Fargo was about to go rummage through the man's saddlebags when a harsh command parted the settlers the way Moses parted the Red Sea.

"Move aside! Make way for Cole Narciss! Stand back, you sluggards, or you'll wish you had!"

Pyle Kutyer barreled through the onlookers with little regard for those he shouldered aside, clearing a path for his employer.

Once, a few years ago, Fargo had seen a visiting duke strut from a fancy carriage into a packed theater, with underlings clearing the way. Cole Narciss reminded him of that pompous duke as Narciss came swaggering up to the body with an assumed air of great importance.

"What have we here?"

"A friend of yours?" Fargo asked, and received a sharp glance from Pyle Kutyer. "He and some friends paid you a visit but you weren't home."

"They were looking for me?" Cole Narciss said, sounding shocked. "What on earth for?"

"You tell me," Fargo responded. He tossed the burlap hood to Wet Grass's leading citizen, who awkwardly caught it.

"What's this? One of their hoods?" Narciss fingered the burlap. "Why is it damp?"

"Blood, would be my guess," Fargo said. "With maybe a little bit of brains mixed in." If he expected Narciss to recoil in shock and drop the hood like it was a red-hot ember, he had misjudged him.

"You don't say? It is about time one of these murdering devils was made to pay." Narciss handed the hood to Pyle Kutyer. "Hold onto that. And collect the dead man's horse. It might furnish a clue as to who he was."

"It's not anyone from hereabouts, Mr. Narciss," someone called out.

"How can this be?" a woman asked. "You have been telling us all along that the night riders had to be from around here."

Narciss held his arms aloft to get their attention. "I am as confounded by this as the rest of you. Be assured, I will get to the bottom of it. In the meantime, you might as well go back to your homes or whatever you were doing. I will personally see to the disposing of the body."

Grumbling occurred, but the crowd slowly dispersed. Some only went as far as the front gate, and huddled in small groups to talk.

"Just what we needed," Pyle Kutyer muttered.

"More unanswered questions?" Cole Narciss quickly said. "Is that what you are upset about?"

A little too quickly, Fargo thought. He nudged the body with a toe. "So you have never set eyes on this gent before?"

"Of course not," Narciss said indignantly. "I am not in the habit of riding around at night with a burlap bag over *my* head."

"Where have you been?" Fargo asked.

"Not that it is any of your business," Narciss answered testily, "but I was with a lady friend."

That reminded Fargo. He had a lady friend of his own to meet. He turned to go.

"Wait. What about our meeting? I wanted to have a few words with you, remember?" Narciss said.

"I'm listening."

"Out here?" Cole Narciss indicated his house. "I would rather present my proposition in the comfort of my parlor, over whiskey and cigars."

"Here will do," Fargo said.

"Very well," Narciss said, but he did not sound happy about it. "I will be brief and to the point." He paused. "How would you like to come work for me?"

To say Fargo was surprised was an understatement. "You're serious?"

"Never more so. You have all the qualities I look for, not the least of which is your skill with a sidearm. And I am a man short, after you went and blew out Greasy Joe's wick. What do you say?"

Fargo did not trust Narciss as far as he could heave Narciss's house. But he did not say that to the man's face.

Apparently construing the silence to mean Fargo was thinking the offer over, Cole Narciss waxed on. "I pay well. Better than you would earn scouting for the military, I assure you. Your job would consist mainly of protecting me and doing certain special tasks from time to time."

"What sort of tasks?" Fargo asked.

Narciss shrugged. "Nothing that would tax a man of your abilities. How about it? Will you at least think it over? You can get back to me in a day or two with your answer."

"It won't take that long," Fargo said. "The answer is no. As soon as I am sure I don't have smallpox, I am fanning the breeze."

"How unfortunate," Narciss said. "But there is always the chance you might reconsider. If so, let me know."

Fargo's no was final but he let the man go on thinking what he wanted. "If that was all you wanted," he said, and wheeled. The skin between his shoulder blades prickled as he walked off. He did not like turning his back to the pair. But he doubted they would do anything with settlers loitering near the picket fence.

Someone called his name from the shadows.

Fargo stopped, his hand close to his Colt. Two figures appeared. One he recognized as John Busby, the farmer he had met in the saloon. Judging by the other man's clothes, he was a farmer, too. "What do you want?"

"This is a friend of mine, Steve Sherwood," Busby said. "His farm is right next to mine."

Fargo remembered Jasmine's comment. "The one who married a dove named Helen Duckers?"

Sherwood had the typical sun-bronzed, weathered features of a tiller of the soil. "Where on earth did you hear about that? But yes, that's me. I am pleased to meet you." He offered his hand.

Another thing about farmers, Fargo mused as he shook, was that hard work gave them hard muscles and a strong grip. "Pleased to meet you." He figured that was all they wanted and went to go on.

"If you don't mind," Sherwood said hastily, "maybe you could stop by my place tomorrow. I have something I would like to talk to you about."

"Why not talk about it here?"

Sherwood glanced anxiously about. "Too many ears. What I have to say is for you and you alone."

"Why me?" Fargo wanted to know.

"John, here, told me who you are. You are just the man we need. Showing up as you have, you are a godsend."

"I'm just passing through." Fargo had no intention of becoming more involved than he had to.

Sherwood and Busby looked at one another, and Sherwood said, "Don't you realize what's at stake? Innocent men, women, and children are being brutally murdered by those bastards in the burlap sacks."

"What is it you think I can do?"

"Put a stop to the slaughter, what else?" Steve Sherwood responded. "You are the only person who can."

"You give me too much credit," Fargo said. "The stories you have heard or read make more of me than there is."

"You are too modest by half," Sherwood said flatly. "Please. Reconsider. At the very least, pay me a visit. I have information that may change your mind."

"I'll see," was as far as Fargo was willing to commit himself. He left the disappointed pair and walked toward the saloon. Absorbed in all that had happened, he was slow to wake up to the fact that he was being followed. Moving his head only slightly, he peered from under his hat brim.

There were two of them. Both were young and brawny. Both wore homespun clothes but store-bought hats. Both wore revolvers. They made no effort at stealth, but stopped when he stopped and moved on when he moved on.

Fargo walked faster. Ahead, mired in darkness, was a gap between the general store and the next building. Darting into it, Fargo put his back to the wall and palmed his Colt. He did not have long to wait. The pair came hurrying past.

"Blazes! Where did he get to?"

"He can't have reached the saloon. We'd have seen him go in."

As stealthily as a stalking cougar, Fargo cat-footed up behind them, raised the Colt, and thumbed back the hammer. "Keep your hands where I can see them."

The two young men became granite sculptures.

Fargo slowly sidled around in front of them. The one on the left had dark hair, the one on the right was showing more teeth than a senator on the stump. "Who are you and why are you following me?"

"I'm Billy Flate," the dark-haired one said. "My pard, here, is Matt Dancer."

"We were hoping to have a word with you," Dancer said.

"Doesn't everyone tonight," Fargo observed. He was becoming more popular than a cure for smallpox. "Do you work for Cole Narciss?"

"Heck, no," Matt Dancer said. "That uppity cuss couldn't pay us enough to work for him."

"He's so mean, he makes sidewinders and gators seem tame," Billy Flate added.

"The fact is," Matt Dancer said, and glanced over his shoulder to be sure he was not overheard, "we would like to hire you to kill him."

6

Fargo had worked at various jobs. He scouted, he tracked, he blazed trails, he hired out as a guide on occasion, and once he even led a cattle drive, but the one thing he did not do—the one thing he never did—was hire out his six-gun. "I'm not an assassin," he informed the pair.

"We're not asking you to make a habit of it," said Matt Dancer. "All we want is for you to kill one man."

"Why don't you kill him yourselves?" Fargo posed the logical question.

Billy Flate answered. "Because we're not assassins, either. I used to trap for fur and hunt gators."

"I was a snake wrangler," Matt Dancer said.

Fargo had never heard of any such thing, and remarked as much.

"Ever hear of a zoo?" Dancer asked. "Those newfangled places where they keep wild critters for folks to admire? One opened up in New Orleans. The old cuss who ran it hired me to go off in the woods and swamps and rustle up snakes for him."

"Just when you think you've heard everything," Fargo said. "What are you two doing here?"

Billy Flate brightened. "We're on our way to California. We heard about the gold rush and reckon we have as much chance as anyone else of striking it rich."

Fargo stared, then said, "The gold rush was twelve years ago."

"We know that," Matt Dancer said, "but we figure there must be plenty of gold still there for the finding."

"So we used all our money to buy a couple of pack-horses and supplies, and came west," Billy Flate took up the account. "We were crossing the Mississippi River when one of our packhorses drowned."

"How did it fall off the ferry?" Fargo asked. He had used those ferries many a time. They had rails to keep accidents like that from happening.

"We didn't use one," Billy Flate said. "They wanted two bits from each of us, the thieves, to cross one measly river."

Matt Dancer nodded. "We figured we could find a place to cross and not have to pay the money."

"The Mississippi is a mile wide in places and has treacherous currents," Fargo mentioned.

"We found that out the hard way," Billy Flate lamented, "when our lead packhorse stepped into a sinkhole and never came up. We had a dickens of a time cutting the rope so the other packhorse wasn't pulled under."

"All our food was on the critter that sank," Matt Dancer lamented. "Our prospecting gear was on the horse I accidentally shot."

"You what?"

"I was cleaning my pistol and the danged thing went off," Matt explained. "Shot that poor horse smack between the eyes. I will never forget the look on its face as it keeled over."

"Most people unload their guns before they clean them," Fargo dryly commented.

"I will the next time, believe you me. Unless it's late and I'm tired. But I'll make darned sure I'm not near any horses."

"Or people," Fargo suggested. "So you lost all your food, and your picks and shovels, and came on anyway?"

"We're not quitters, mister," Billy Flate said. "When we put our minds to something, we see it through."

"Except wrangling snakes," Matt Dancer said. "It wasn't as much fun as I thought it would be. Them pesky serpents wriggle and hiss and like to bite."

"Have you ever thought of maybe being store clerks?"

Billy Flate arched an eyebrow. "Why in God's name

would we want to do that? Clerking is dull. And I'd look funny in one of those silly aprons. It'd be like that time I put on my sister's dress."

"We're hankering for excitement," Billy Dancer said. "We want to do all the stuff folks talk about. Hunt a griz, shoot buffalo, tangle with hostiles."

"You might want to rethink the hostiles," Fargo advised. "I figure you would last about four seconds."

"We can take care of ourselves!" Billy Flate declared. "Watch this." His hand dropped to his revolver and he jerked it from his holster. Somehow he snagged the barrel as he drew and the six-shooter flipped from his grasp and landed in the street at his feet, raising tiny swirls of dust. "Dang. Did that again."

"Would you like to see me draw?" Matt Dancer asked.

"What I would really like is a drink." Fargo started for the saloon.

"Hold on," Billy Flate said. "You haven't heard the rest of it. How we stumbled across this godforsaken gob of spit, and now that Cole Narciss won't let us leave on account of the smallpox."

"That's why you want me to shoot him?"

"I would do it but there's something wrong with my pistol," Matt Dancer said. "It never hits where I aim it."

"You really won't take the job?" Billy Flate asked. "Not even for ten dollars?"

"Top assassins hire out for a thousand dollars or more, I've heard," Fargo made mention.

"But you said yourself you don't kill folks for a living," Matt Dancer responded. "You should do it for cheap."

"Besides, ten dollars is half of all we have left," Billy said. "Which is another reason we want to light a shuck."

"The answer is still no." Fargo figured that was the end of it and moved on, but they came up on either side of him, as persistent as terriers.

"Won't you reconsider?" Matt Dancer asked. "We'll give you a thousand once we strike it rich."

"Shouldn't take us no time to find gold," Billy Flate predicted. "Provided we don't take a wrong turn somewhere and end up in Oregon instead of California."

Fargo entered the saloon. The place was doing brisk business. Jim and Jackie Fina were busily serving drinks and food. Many of the crowd that had gathered at Narciss's house had repaired to the saloon to talk about the shooting and other developments. Cat Sultraine and Pinky Belle moved among them, all smiles and willowy charm.

A silence fell when Fargo appeared. Every eye swung toward him. Whispers and murmurs followed him to the far end of the bar. Without being asked, Jim Fina brought a bottle and a glass.

Fargo filled the glass to the brim and downed the red-eye in a single gulp. The two young gold seekers, Flate and Dancer, had strayed over to a table and were talking to others. He refilled the glass and was raising it to his lips when perfume wreathed him like a cloud and a warm form pressed against his side.

"Here you are!" Jasmine cooed softly in his ear. "I was beginning to worry I might not get to see you. Word is, you shot someone."

Fargo shifted and looped an arm around Jasmine's slender waist. "It seemed like the right thing to do at the time."

"I have good news," Jasmine said. "Jim is letting me off early. Another half an hour and I am yours." She pecked him on the cheek. "Don't you go anywhere, you hear?" Her hips swaying invitingly, she moseyed off.

Fargo downed more whiskey. Now that he thought about it, seven to ten more days in Wet Grass held little appeal, other than the ladies. Their appeal was considerable, but he also needed to be in St. Louis by the end of the month. Instead of waiting around, he would head for St. Louis, staying well clear of the Oregon Trail so he would not come into contact with anyone, and if he did not come down with smallpox, he would arrive on time. If he did contract the disease, he would be no worse off than he would in Wet Grass, which lacked a doctor.

The more Fargo thought about it, the more he liked the idea. He would leave in the morning and stop by the Sherwood farm on his way out. By noon, Wet Grass would be well behind him, and good riddance.

Fargo had done justice to a third of the bottle when

he sensed that someone had come up close to him. He shifted, expecting to see Jasmine.

The three slabs of human beef confronting him wore scowls of anger. They were near-identical in size and shape except that one had a square jaw, one had big ears, and the third had a crooked nose.

"Remember us?" said the slab with the square jaw.

"You were with Pyle Kutyer and Greasy Joe at the Sunman place," Fargo recollected.

"That's us," big ears declared.

"Greasy Joe was our pard," remarked the hardcase with the crooked nose. "We don't like what you did to him."

"He didn't leave me much breathing space," Fargo reminded them.

The man with the square jaw smiled sadistically. "We're not going to leave you any, either."

"But we'll be smart about it," said big ears. "We're not going to go for our hardware. We've seen how fast you are."

Crooked nose tittered. "That's right. We're fixing to pound you into the floor with out fists and our feet."

"Is that so?" Fargo filled his glass and set the bottle down, but did not take his hand off it. "What would Cole Narciss say?"

"Who gives a damn?" snapped big ears. "He pays us to bust heads, not lick his boots. This is personal."

The man with the square jaw motioned. "We don't want to beat on you in here. Some idiot might take it into their noggin to help you."

"We'll follow you out," crooked nose said. "Just keep your hands where we can see them."

"What if I don't want to go?"

"Can you count, mister?" big ears rasped. "There are three of us and only one of you. Don't do anything to make us madder than we are."

"Like this?" Fargo spun, and swung. The bottle met big ears's temple and shattered. Spinning again, Fargo planted his fist in crooked nose's gut. That left square jaw, who howled in outrage and closed in.

Startled cries greeted the sudden violence. Men scrambled to make room. Jim Fina reached under the bar and brought out a club, but he was at the other end. "Stop that, you hear!" he shouted.

Fargo met square jaw head-on. He blocked a punch to the throat and unleashed an uppercut that started down near the floor. The blow lifted square jaw off the floor and bent him into a bow. Crashing down, he lay still.

"Damn you!" Crooked nose was up and lunging. He was a grappler, and held his arms wide.

Fargo sprang back just as those arms closed. His fists jabbed in lightning sequence, rocking crooked nose on his heels. The man raised his arms to protect himself. Fargo slipped a block and landed a cross that snapped crooked nose's head around. Bellowing in fury, crooked nose forgot himself and sought to grapple again, only to be met with a jolting blow to the cheek that split it like so much ripe fruit.

Snarling, crooked nose dived at Fargo's legs. Fargo sidestepped but a shoulder jarred him sufficiently to send him tottering. Before he could regain his balance, big ears attacked. Big ears had recovered from the bottle to the temple, and unexpectedly reared up behind Fargo, seizing him by the arms and pinning them.

"I've got him, Ben! Give him what for!"

Ben was the one with the crooked nose. Grinning, he said, "Here's where you get yours, mister." He set himself and cocked his fist. "Hold him still, Darnell."

Fargo tensed and braced his legs.

"How does it feel, mister?" Darnell hollered. "Knowing we're fixing to bust every bone in your body, and there's not a damn thing you can do about it!"

"I'll commence with your nose," Ben said, and drove his fist forward.

Fargo pivoted at the hip. He threw all his weight and every ounce of strength in his steely sinews into the swing. Darnell, caught unprepared, yelped as he was whipped bodily around so he was between Fargo and Ben. The blow intended for Fargo's nose connected with

Darnell's spine instead, and Darnell howled in pain. His grip slackened, and the next instant Fargo had thrown him off and retreated to give himself room to move.

"I'm sorry. I'm sorry. I'm sorry," Ben kept saying over and over as he helped his partner to stay on his feet. "The son of a bitch is trickier than a fox."

"There are still two of us," Darnell grunted. "I'll go right, you go left, and we'll catch him between us."

Fargo was grateful for the information. As they stalked toward him, he backed away. Since they made no move for weapons, neither did he. The patrons had vacated the vicinity and were pressed together over near the window and the door.

Jim Fina started to come around the end of the bar but Darnell jabbed a finger at him and growled, "Butt in, and you're liable to spend the next six months on crutches. This is between us and him."

Fargo bumped something. A glance showed it to be a chair. Stopping, he waited.

Ben crouched and slid warily forward on the balls of his feet. "I'll take him low, pard, you take him high."

At a nod from Darnell, they sprang.

Whirling, Fargo gripped the chair. It described a tight arc that ended with a resounding crash as it splintered against Darnell's head. Almost in the same heartbeat, Fargo snapped his knee into Ben's face. The crunch of Ben's crooked nose was drowned out by his howl, and the howl was silenced by a solid right to the jaw.

A hand fell on Fargo's shoulder and he spun, but it was Cat Sultraine. Her pouty lips puckered in a smile.

"My oh my. You sure are a wildcat. I hope you are the same in bed."

Pinky Belle came up beside her. "I bet he has a lot of muscles under those buckskins. A lot of hair, too."

Jasmine hooked Fargo's arm in hers and wagged a finger at her friends. "I have him first, remember? You two hussies take cold baths and wait your turn." She pulled him toward the door. "I'm ready if you are."

Fargo was more than ready.

7

Jasmine Keller's apartment was typical of most doves. Small but comfortable, it was the best she could afford.

No sooner did Fargo close the door than the saucy redhead hungrily molded her luscious body to his and fused her mouth to his in a wet, warm kiss that went on and on and on.

When they finally parted for breath, Fargo grinned and said, "Starved for affection, are you?"

"You have no idea, handsome," Jasmine languidly replied while running her hands up and down his arms, sculpting the hard muscles. "Most of the farmers and settlers are married. They don't dare touch us working girls or there will be hell to pay with their wives. Take John Busby. If he so much as talks to us, he's in the doghouse. Then there are those like, say, Glenn Handy, who are friendly as can be, but love their wives too much to ever trifle with another filly."

"What about the ones who aren't married?"

"Not many are the kind a girl wants to bring home. There was one nice fella, Steve Sherwood, who acted like we were his own private bordello, but then he went and got hitched to Helen Duckers, and now the only one he does is her."

Fargo had a sudden thought. "Does Mr. High-and-mighty treat himself?"

"Cole Narciss?" Jasmine puckered her brow. "He's a strange one. He treats us like we're his property. Oh, he doesn't hit us or anything like that. But he doesn't touch any of us any other way, if you get what I mean."

"Not ever?"

"He showed an interest in a rich widow on a wagon train once," Jasmine related. "But she was the only female I've ever seen or heard of him cottoning to."

"What about the men who work for him?"

"As randy as goats. But I wouldn't bring any of them here. Not even Pyle Kutyer. He's good-looking, but I suspect he's the type who would want me to tie him to the bed and whip him with a belt. I don't need that, thank you."

"Speaking of tying, you've never been tempted to tie the knot, yourself?"

Jasmine smiled rather sadly. "That's every dove's dream. Don't ever kid yourself it isn't." She paused. "A while back there was this gent I was fond of. Burt Stevens. Just when I was warming up to him, he ran off and joined the army." She stopped, then giggled.

"What?"

"Oh, nothing. There are these two young ones who showed up recently. They fawn over us ladies like we're fine china. But they know next to nothing about women."

Fargo had a hunch who she was talking about. "What man does?"

"You have a point. Most men are as ignorant as tree stumps when it comes to females. But these two are in a world all their own. One of them, Matt Dancer, wanted to know if women can twine themselves up like snakes when they make love. And his friend, Billy Flate, likes to puff on a girl's navel as though we're some kind of balloon. Can you imagine?"

"I've met them," Fargo mentioned. He was about to attach his lips to her neck when she rambled on.

"Don't let me give you the wrong notion. Before the smallpox struck, Wet Grass was better than most places. At least the married ladies don't outright hate us. A few, like a gal named Lori Gan, treat us just like they would anyone else."

"That's nice," Fargo said, for lack of anything better.

"There's even a gal who runs a farm by herself. Sally Franklin. She can hold her own with any man, and probably lick nine of out ten without working up a sweat."

Fargo had about as much interest in the various settlers as he did in the mating habits of flamingos. Jasmine could babble if she wanted, but he was stirring, low down, and had other things in mind. Pressing his mouth to her throat, he licked a path to an ear and sucked on the lobe.

"Mmm," Jasmine breathed. "I guess you don't want to talk. Which is fine. Keep doing what you're doing. I'm sensitive there."

Other places too, Fargo soon learned. He kissed her chin, her eyebrows, her mouth, the while slowly steering her toward the bed. She responded in kind. Her body grew warmer. Her cheeks became flushed. When he cupped her bottom and ground against her, a soft moan fluttered from her throat.

The bed was small but covered with a thick, soft quilt. Sinking onto it was like sinking into a cushion of silk. Fargo stretched out next to Jasmine. He started to slide his knee along her leg, then sat up. "Just a minute." He began to remove his boots.

"That's not necessary," Jasmine said.

"Unless you want my spurs to rip this quilt of yours to shreds, it is," Fargo replied.

"Oh. Usually I have men take them off before we fool around." Jasmine took his hat, set it on the floor, and playfully ran her fingers through his hair. "You have me so excited, I plumb forgot."

Fargo was tugging off his second boot when he thought he heard a sound out in the hallway. A sound so faint he could not tell what it was. He listened but it was not repeated, so he turned back to Jasmine. Hers was not the only apartment. He took it for granted that the sound had been one of the other tenants. "Now where were we?"

"Here," Jasmine said. Her tongue slid between her parted lips to meet his in a silken swirl.

With his right hand Fargo explored her voluptuous body, while with his left he worked on the buttons and stays that would bare her charms once her clothes were shed. Some women had a fondness for buttons and stays, and undressing them took forever. Jasmine, to his delight, was not one of them. In fact, her dress had fewer than any dress he had ever come across. Purposely so, he reckoned. He bunched the upper half down around her waist and hiked at the bottom half until it was bunched with the rest. Thankfully, she did not wear petticoats or a crinoline. Her cotton chemise and drawers were easily attended to. Then there they were, Jasmine's breasts, bare and full and ripe, twin melons waiting to be tasted. Fargo inhaled a nipple and nipped it lightly with his teeth. It provoked a shiver.

Jasmine tugged at his shirt. She had to struggle some to get it off. As she cast it aside, her eyes widened. "My goodness. What a body you have. There's not an ounce of flab anywhere." She eagerly ran her hands over his chest and washboard stomach.

Cupping her breasts, Fargo kneaded them like clay. She wriggled and sighed, then bit her lip to stifle an outcry when he pinched both nipples at once. He traced his tongue from her mounds to her navel, and remembering what she had said a few minutes ago, puffed on it.

Jasmine's body shook with quiet mirth.

Easing her under him, Fargo knelt between her long legs. Her thighs, as smooth as satin and as soft as down, merited attention. He caressed and stroked them for several minutes.

"You sure know how to make a girl tingle," Jasmine complimented him.

"There are a lot more tingles to come," Fargo promised, and a moment later covered her mount with his palm. At the contact she arched her back and her legs opened and closed, her ankles hooking behind him.

"I can't wait. Do me. Do me now."

Fargo was in no great hurry. He ran his forefinger along her moist slit, parting her nether lips. Jasmine came up off the bed as if she were trying to leap to the ceiling.

She moaned, long and loud, and her thighs wrapped tighter.

Lavishing more kisses on her face and neck, Fargo slowly inserted his finger into her molten core. She was hot for him, hot and wet and yielding. When he added a second finger, her nails dug into his shoulders fit to rip off skin. They dug deeper still when he lightly glided his finger across her swollen knob. He began pumping his two fingers. She responded by churning her hips. As his fingers moved faster, so did her hips. Suddenly she threw her head back and groaned. Her body went into paroxysms of release. It was a while before she subsided and lay panting for breath.

"Dang. You're good."

Fargo rose on his knees, reached down, and aligned his member with her womanhood. "There's more to come."

Her eyes hooded in wanton lust, Jasmine regarded his engorged pole much as a starved person might regard a loaf of bread. "I had no idea you have so much in common with a bull buffalo."

Chuckling, Fargo rubbed the tip of his staff along her slit. She quivered again, and the pink tip of her tongue appeared between her red lips. "Like that, do you?"

"More than you will ever know," Jasmine husked. "If I ever find the right man, I will do this every day of the week and twice on Saturdays."

Some lucky hombre, Fargo reflected, was in for a treat. He slowly inserted his pulsing sword into her velvet sheath. Her inner walls were incredibly soft and yielding. They clung to him like a wet glove. When he moved, they rippled and contracted, inducing waves of pleasure.

"Like that, lover. Just like that," Jasmine cooed.

Placing his hands on her hips, Fargo commenced to drive up into her with ever faster, ever harder strokes. She bucked like a bronc, matching his vigor, his ardor. She was a mare to his stallion, craving him as fully as he craved her.

The bed creaking under them, Fargo leaned back, relishing the sensation. He started to close his eyes, then snapped them open again. He thought he had seen a face at the window, peering in through a crack in the curtains. But it was gone. Fargo tensed, waiting for the face to reappear.

"What's wrong?" Jasmine mewed. "Why did you stop?"

Fargo hadn't realized he had. He resumed thrusting into her, his gaze never leaving the glass pane. Only after a couple of minutes had gone by was he satisfied that it had been a trick of the light cast by Jasmine's small lamp.

"Harder!" she took that second to urge. "I want it harder!'

Fargo obliged, ramming into her over and over. His mouth devoured her lips, her breasts, her nipples. Their mutual need climbed. Their sensual frenzy soared. And then, at the apex of their lust, Jasmine cried out and shook with the carnal violence of release.

"Oh! Oh! I'm there!"

Her cry was the spark that ignited Fargo's own inner fire. His body a bubbling cauldron, he crested. Afterward came the gradual floating down from the heights of ecstasy to the reality of the sweat-caked body under him. Spent, he rolled onto his side and draped an arm across her bosom.

"You were magnificent," Jasmine praised him in a hoarse whisper. "The best I ever had."

Fargo suspected she said that to all her men. But he prudently kept the thought to himself. Lethargy seized him and spread through his veins. He was close to dozing off when she made a comment that shattered the cloud he was floating on.

"I better get some sleep. I need to be up early. I want to visit the pen where Narciss is keeping those folks who might have smallpox. I hear that some of the women and children are in a bad way, so I'm going to ask Narciss if I can take them some food."

"Kids are in there, too?"

"Anyone and everyone who has been exposed. Most of us don't like it much, but there's not anything we can do, what with Pyle Kutyer and those others Narciss has working for him."

Fargo rose onto an elbow. "I'd like to tag along." He wanted to see this pen for himself.

"You are more than welcome," Jasmine said. "But we won't be able to get too close. If we do, we'll be thrown in the pen ourselves."

"How will you get the food to them, then?"

"The guards handle that. They have a way of doing it so no one else can come down with the disease. You'll see for yourself." Jasmine paused and gave him a searching scrutiny. "That business at Narciss's house tonight. What did you make of it?"

"The man I shot wasn't a farmer or from Wet Grass."

"Yes. So I've heard. But that's not what I meant. Why were the night riders after Cole Narciss?"

Fargo shrugged. "Your guess is as good as mine. There's a lot about this that doesn't make much sense."

"Everyone is talking," Jasmine said. "They think the night riders were out to kill him."

"What reason would they have?"

"Because he is the only one who has any chance of stopping them," Jasmine said. "He has nine men working for him, counting Pyle. With him dead, the others will leave, and the night riders can do as they please."

Fargo mulled that over a while. He was not satisfied that was the answer. But he could see why the settlers might think so.

"I just want the nightmare to end," Jasmine remarked. "Sooner or later the smallpox will run its course and then everything will be as it was."

"Why hasn't someone ridden to Fort Kearney for the doctor?" Fargo happened to know there was one assigned to the post, a competent major with the unusual name of Spyder.

"Two people tried. One was a lady called Libby whose husband was thrown into the pen. The second was a man named Jason, from here in Wet Grass. Neither was ever seen again. Hostiles were to blame, most everyone figures." Jasmine yawned. "No one has tried since."

Fargo happened to have his back to the door. He did not hear it open, but he did see the sudden fear that

52

sprouted in Jasmine's eyes. Instantly, he started to rise and turn, and reached for his Colt.

"I wouldn't, were I you."

"Leave the hogleg where it is, mister."

Three men had slipped into the apartment as stealthily as specters. All three wore burlap sacks with eyeholes and slits for their mouths. Under other circumstances they would seem comical. But there was nothing comical about the revolvers they leveled at the bed.

"Night riders!" Jasmine exclaimed.

"No fooling," one of the hooded figures retorted. "It goes without saying, I trust, that if either of you lets out a peep, you're dead."

8

Even though three revolvers were pointed in his direction, Fargo almost leaped at the night riders. They would not expect it and, if he moved fast enough, they might not get off a shot. Then again, if they did, there was Jasmine to think of. She was bound to take a stray slug if lead started flying. So Fargo did the only thing he could; he raised his hands, and lied. "I won't give you any trouble."

The stockiest of the night riders swaggered forward. "Nice to see someone with some common sense for a change." As wary as if he were dealing with a coiled rattler, the man plucked Fargo's Colt from its holster. "Keep on behaving and you'll live a while longer."

Jasmine pulled on the quilt to cover herself, but it only came as high as her waist because she was sitting on it. Crossing her forearms over her breasts, she snapped, "How dare you come in here uninvited! What is the meaning of this outrage? What do you think you are doing?"

"The same as always," the stocky night rider said. "We're keeping the good people of Wet Grass safe from the smallpox."

"Neither of us have it," Jasmine said. "I demand that the three of you leave this instant!"

"Sorry, lady," the man said. "But this friend of yours was exposed at the Sunman farm. Or didn't he tell you?"

"I helped dig the graves," Fargo said.

"That's all?" Jasmine pulled on the quilt again, without any result. Frustrated, she snatched up a pillow and held it in front of her.

The three burlap bags swiveled toward her. The men wearing them were more interested in her antics, or her lack of attire, than they were in Fargo. The man who had been doing the most talking now chortled and remarked, "Ain't she a sight, boys? I haven't seen jugs that big in a coon's age."

"You are uncouth," Jasmine said.

"Hell, I don't even know what that words means," the night rider replied. "But if it means I like naked women, then that's me in spades." He nudged a companion with an elbow. "How would you like to get your hands on that body of hers? I could pound her for hours."

Fargo elected to do some pounding of his own. Amazingly, they were paying no attention to him. They seemed to take it for granted that he would stand there as meek as a lamb while they ogled Jasmine. They were mistaken.

Because of the hoods over their heads, Fargo could not tell where their jaws were. So he compromised. He was in among them before they could react and smashed his fist into the center of the stocky man's hood. The man yelped and staggered but did not go down. The other two, as Fargo anticipated, swung toward him, and the twin clicks of twin hammers warned him he was a heartbeat from being hurled into eternity. He lashed out with both arms, swatting their revolvers aside. Neither fired. But leaping back, they took deliberate aim.

The stocky night rider, recovering sufficiently, croaked through the burlap, "No shooting, damn you! We're to take him alive, remember!"

Fargo had seldom heard more welcome news. He waded into the two in front of him. A barrel flashed at his head, but he ducked and retaliated with a solid right cross that slammed the man against a wall. The other one relied on his fist. Fargo sidestepped, felt knuckles graze his cheek, and uncorked a combination that dropped the man to his knees.

The stocky night rider chose that moment to reenter the fray. Only he used his wits, not his brawn. "Feel this?"

Fargo did, and turned to stone. A muzzle was jammed hard against his backbone. If the six-shooter went off, his spine would be blown in half.

"The boss wants you brought back alive," the stocky man said. "But he also told us to do whatever we have to if you won't go along quietly, so what will it be? Quiet as a mouse or with a few bullet holes in you?"

"Quiet has its appeal," Fargo said.

The man laughed harshly. "I figured it would." He motioned at one of the others. "Check the hallway. We can do without bumping into any Good Samaritans."

Jasmine had risen on her knees, exposing more of her luscious figure. "Hold on! Try taking him and I will scream!"

"Scream and I will by God shoot anyone who tries to stop us," the stocky night rider warned.

Jasmine wrung her hands in the quilt. "What do I do?" she asked Fargo.

"Get dressed. I'll be back as soon as I can."

All three night riders chuckled at that. The stocky one gouged Fargo with his revolver, and said, "You like to look at the bright sides of things, I take it? Well, mister, I wouldn't get my hopes up, were I you."

At gunpoint Fargo was prodded along the hall and down the stairs at the rear. Naked from the waist up, and in his stockinged feet, Fargo fought off fleeting despair. He hoped to heaven none of the night riders glanced at his feet. He still had the Arkansas toothpick, and with every step he took, the bottom of his pant leg rose half an inch or so, enough to expose the bottom of the sheath.

The stocky man was gloating. "You weren't as tough to take as the boss figured you would be."

"Who is this boss you keep mentioning?" Fargo quizzed him.

"If he wants you to know, he will tell you himself." The stocky night rider gave Fargo a push. "The thing for

56

you to worry about is what I'm going to do to you when he says I can."

Four horses were waiting. The Ovaro was not one of them. Fargo was hustled to a zebra dun and instructed to mount. Two men covered him. They did not climb on their horses until the stocky man had climbed on his and could watch Fargo.

"You might be thinking you can get away. That all you have to do is wait for the right moment and give that zebra dun its head. Think again. All I have to do is whistle a certain whistle and that dun will come to a stop. Savvy?"

They rode north, toward the river. The night was alive with life: the shrill yips of coyotes, the piercing screech of an owl, the croak of frogs, and the chirp of crickets. The vegetation that fringed the Platte was thick. Timber grew in profusion. Without a good sense of direction, a man could easily get lost. But Fargo's abductors knew exactly how to get where they were going.

It was a clearing thirty feet across, lit by a small campfire. The dozen-plus hooded figures parted so Fargo and his escorts could ride right up to the fire.

"Look who it is," declared the apparent leader. "You did good, boys. One less headache for us to deal with."

Fargo tried to identify the speaker by his voice, but it was muffled by the burlap. He had the impression the man was further disguising it somehow. "Takes a brave man to hide behind a hood like you're doing."

The man in charge gestured, and four others sprang to pull Fargo from the zebra dun. Fargo kicked and caught one in the chest. Two more immediately jumped to help. Fargo's arms and legs were seized in vise grips he could not break, and he was slammed onto his back.

In the flickering glow of the fire it all seemed unreal. The dancing shadows, the spectral forms, their bizarre hoods. Fargo wondered if he should pinch himself. Then the leader loomed over him.

"I don't like meddlers."

"Is that what I've been doing?" Fargo baited him, and paid for it with a brutal kick below the belt. Pain exploded through every particle of his being. He gritted his teeth, but could not keep from gasping and sputtering.

"That is a taste of what you will get if you don't rein in that mouth of yours," the leader stated. "You have meddled in something you shouldn't have, and you must be held to account."

"I'm only passing through," Fargo said.

"So you say. But we have our doubts. Some of us have heard of you. Heard that you are a famous scout, like Kit Carson."

The pain had peaked. Fargo controlled it with considerable effort and responded, "So?"

"So you have worked for the army from time to time," the leader said. He leaned down. "What we want to know is whether you are working for the army now."

"What difference would that make?" Fargo rejoined. The army had no jurisdiction in civilian matters except in rare instances.

The leader drew back his leg to kick but did not follow through. "We don't want the government sticking its big nose in, is all."

"They have no idea what is going on here," Fargo said.

The leader straightened. "If only we could believe you."

"Is that all you wanted?" Fargo demanded. "Is that why you dragged me out here?" He was mad. Mad enough to tear into them, guns or no guns.

"That is part of it," the leader said. "We also have learned that you were exposed to smallpox at the Sunman farm. That makes you a danger to everyone else."

"I never touched the bodies."

"But you were there, and they died of smallpox, and that's enough," the leader said. "Which is why we are going to throw you into the pen with the rest of those who have been exposed."

"Like hell you are," Fargo said. His risk of contracting the disease would be higher among others who had possibly been exposed.

"It's not as if you have a say. We decide who is and isn't quarantined."

"You don't have the right."

"Our lives are at stake. That gives us all the right we need." The leader sniffed. "All the right *I* need."

"Enjoy playing the Almighty while you can," Fargo said.

The tall figure was still a few seconds. "Is that what you think this is? Delusions of grandeur, as they say? You couldn't be more wrong. There is more at stake than you can possibly imagine. But I've said too much." He addressed the three men who had brought Fargo there. "You know what to do. Get to it."

"We should just shoot the son of a bitch," a night rider muttered.

Whirling, their leader seemed to swell in stature. "Are you in charge now? Do you think you know what's best?"

"No, of course not," the man hastily backed down, traces of genuine fear in his tone. "But he's trouble we don't need."

"Which is why he's being thrown in the pen with the rest of them," the leader said. "If the army or the law ever come around, it will all seem perfectly natural."

Fargo wondered about that remark.

It drew laughs and chortles, which, strangely enough, made their leader angry. "Enough, damn it! You'll give everything away." He pointed at the three men. "Get going. When you're done, rejoin us at the usual place."

Rough hands seized Fargo under his shoulders and half carried, half dragged him to the zebra dun.

"Get on the damn cayuse."

Fargo hooked his toes in the stirrup and swung up. The three night riders turned to climb back on their own mounts, and he chose that moment to say, "If any of you are from around here, I'll eat my hat." All three stopped and faced him.

"Fish all you want," the stocky man said. "We won't take the bait."

"We're farmers, all of us," another said.

"You're a damn liar," Fargo told him. Farmers wore homespun, not store-bought, clothes. Farmers did not go around with revolvers and knives around their waists. And farmers always had calloused, scarred hands from endless hours of hard toil.

"Call me that again and I'll see how many teeth I can knock out with one punch," the man snapped.

"What is it you think you know?" the stocky one asked.

Fargo did not answer.

"I didn't think so," the man said. "You're shooting in the dark. You're no threat to us at all."

Suddenly the leader was beside them. "What's the holdup? Why haven't you left yet?"

"He's been flapping his gums," the stocky one said. "Trying to get us to tell him stuff."

"Ignore him," the leader commanded. "At least *pretend* you are competent. Climb on those nags and light a shuck. *Now*." He stormed toward the fire.

Low curses came from under the hood of the man who had been put in his place. "I hate how that guy acts like he's better than everybody."

"Don't let him hear you say that," advised one of the others.

"Not unless you can breathe dirt," said the third.

"He doesn't worry me half as much as—" The stocky man caught himself. He gestured at his companions. "Enough jabber. Mount up."

Once again they turned toward their mounts. Their backs were to Fargo. None of the other night riders were paying any attention. The leader was hunkered by the fire.

It was an opportunity Fargo could not let slip by. Shrieking like a Comanche, he jabbed his heels again the zebra dun. The dun plowed into the three and sent them sprawling. Another moment, and he was at the edge of the clearing and plunging into the trees.

Yells and oaths were hurled after him.

Bending low, Fargo lashed the reins. Riding pell-mell through a forest at night was fraught with perils, including low limbs, one of which he ducked under with barely a whisker's width to spare. He glanced back.

The leader was roaring commands and shoving others right and left. Night riders were scrambling for their animals. Already half a dozen were wheeling their mounts to give chase.

Fargo concentrated on his riding. He barely saw a log in time to vault it. He had a sizeable lead, but not a safe one. He was still in pistol range. Fortunately, they wanted him alive. Or so he thought until a revolver cracked several times and the air around him was blistered by hot lead.

9

The leader's bellow whipped on the wind. "No shooting, damn your hides! How many times do I have to tell you? We can't have any bullet holes in him!"

Fargo was puzzled by the comment. Whether he died of smallpox or lead, he would still be dead. Then he recalled the remark about the army and the law. It could be, Fargo speculated, the vigilantes were worried that bullet holes would arouse suspicion if his body was ever dug up and examined.

Another low limb abruptly put an end to Fargo's musing. He risked another glance back. The zebra dun had increased its lead, although not by much. It wasn't the Ovaro. But it would, Fargo hoped, do better on open ground. In a few hundred feet he would be out of the woods and there would be nothing but grass until he came to the settlement.

One of the night riders was shouting but Fargo did not catch what the man was saying. He did hear the leader's reply.

"He'll find out soon enough! Be ready! Once we have him, he goes straight to the smallpox pen!"

Fargo did not like the sound of that. The night riders were too sure of themselves, too confident they would catch him.

The last of the trees and underbrush flew past and Fargo goaded the zebra dun to greater speed. Or tried to. For, although he used the reins and his legs like a madman, the zebra dun would not go any faster. It was at its limit, galloping as swiftly as it was capable of.

Fargo tried to tell himself it was fast enough to stay ahead of the night riders. And it appeared to be, at first. The vigilantes were strung out in a line several hundred yards behind him. There was no shouting, no useless threats. They did not try to overtake him.

Which troubled Fargo. Plainly, the faster horses were being held back. Which made no sense, since the last thing the night riders wanted was for him to reach Wet Grass.

The explanation presented itself about the same time the lights of the settlement glimmered on the horizon.

The zebra dun began to slow.

Fargo used the reins and his legs some more, but the animal did not respond. It was breathing heavily and showed every sign of being under great strain.

The night riders had noticed. Some of them laughed.

The truth hit Fargo like a punch to the gut.

Like people, no two horses were alike. Some were faster than others. Some had more endurance. Some horses, and the Ovaro was an example, possessed both speed and stamina. Other horses were not as gifted. Some possessed no stamina whatsoever. They became winded after exerting themselves for a short distance.

The zebra dun was one of the latter.

Fargo continued to lash the reins but he was deluding himself. The zebra dun slowed from a gallop to a trot. It was then that Fargo heard the drum of hooves coming up on either side of him. He twisted right and left. Two night riders on fast mounts were rapidly closing on him. Each night rider was waving an arm over his head.

Swearing under his breath, Fargo tried one last time to goad the zebra dun, but he might as well have goaded a turtle. He put a hand on the saddle horn, about to push off and take his chances on foot, when a swishing noise confirmed what he had suspected. Those men had not been moving their arms for the hell of it.

The next instant a rope settled over Fargo's head and

shoulders. He reached to tear it off but a second loop descended, pinning his arms, and a second later he was wrenched from the saddle.

For a few fleeting moments, Fargo seemed to fly backward. The jolt of crashing to the ground took his breath away. He struggled to shed the ropes but they were too tight.

The two night riders moved in. A revolver glinted dully in the starlight, and the hooded figured on the left said, "We can drag you until all the fight is out of you, or you can lie still. Which will it be?"

Fargo subsided.

A ring of night riders surrounded him. The leader dismounted, stepped up, and kicked him in the side. New agony coursed through him, and Fargo doubled over.

"Try that again and I will have them break your legs," the leader said icily. To the others he snapped, "Bind him. Not just his wrists and his ankles. Wrap a rope around him from his knees to his chest." He turned to climb back on his horse, and snapped his fingers as if he had remembered something. "A gag, too, so he can't squawk. We've wasted enough time with him."

It was not long before coils of rope held Fargo in an inescapable cocoon. A night rider removed his bandanna and jammed it into Fargo's mouth. Fargo tasted the man's sweat and nearly gagged. Another bandanna was tied around his mouth to keep the first bandanna wedged in. He was thrown belly-down over a horse, but not the zebra dun.

The leader took the reins and led the animal over to the same three he had instructed to take Fargo to the pen earlier. "Here." He held out the reins. "Do you suppose you can hold onto him this time?"

"He's a tricky coon," the stocky man who usually did the talking responded.

"And I am a mad one. Make me any madder and you will wish you never set eyes on me."

The trio were silent as they led Fargo to the south. After a while they swung to the east to skirt Wet Grass.

Fargo tried to work the gag loose but the knots were too tight. They came to the Oregon Trail and crossed it. Then it was out across the vast prairie beyond.

The night rider in the lead, the one holding the rope to the horse bearing Fargo, uttered a string of low oaths. "The nerve of that son of a bitch. Talking to me like he did."

"Are you still fuming over that?" the second rider asked.

"We had it coming," said the third. "It was our mistake."

"That doesn't give him the right to treat us like yacks!" groused the lead rider. "What's he ever done, I ask you? Hell, he might be slow as molasses. I've never seen him draw."

"Have a care," cautioned the second man. "He doesn't need to be good with a revolver when he can hire others who are to do his killing."

"Hell, I ain't scared of him," the first man blustered. "Not him, nor anything in britches, neither."

"Let it rest," the second man said.

The third night rider piped up with, "One day that gum flapping of yours will be the death of you."

Fargo had been listening closely to their voices. He was virtually certain they were the three men who had tried to beat his brains out in the saloon. The stocky rider was Ben, the hardcase with the crooked nose. The second rider was Darnell, the one with the big ears. Fargo could not recall hearing the name of the third. If he was right, it confirmed what he had already suspected.

In a while they bore more to the west. The lights of the settlement were now north of them. Someone had mentioned that the smallpox pen was a mile south of Wet Grass, and before long Fargo spied a campfire about where the pen should be.

Ben and his friends drew rein. Ben handed the rope to Darnell, then rode at a walk toward the campfire.

"I'm glad we don't have to get any closer," the third night rider whispered.

"That place spooks me."

"What the hell for?" Darnell said. "It's not as if you can catch the pox."

The third man glanced sharply at Fargo, then said, "Even so, I can't stand to look at those folks."

"I gave you credit for more sand," Darnell criticized.

"It's not that. I'll swap lead or steel with any hombre this side of the Rio Grande, and give as good as I get. But shooting a man is one thing. Watching him waste away is another."

"It doesn't bother me none," Darnell said. "Still, I'll be glad when this business is over with. It goes against my grain to skulk around in the dark wearing these stupid hoods."

"Yours and mine, both," the third night rider said. "When we hired on there was no mention of this silliness."

"He should just gun them down and be done with it," Darnell declared. "But I reckon he's smart to do it so the law can't touch him. There's nothing worse than doing a strangulation jig."

"You can't hang smallpox."

Both men laughed.

Fargo hoped they would go on talking, maybe give more away, but they became clams. Presently, Ben returned. Without saying a word, he took the rope from Darnell, wrapped it around the saddle horn, then gave the horse Fargo was draped over a smack on the flank.

The animal trotted toward the campfire.

By craning his neck, Fargo saw four men armed with rifles waiting for the horse. It was only when he came into the glow cast by the flickering flames that Fargo glimpsed the outline of something he could not quite identify in the darkness past the fire.

The four men had bandannas over their noses and mouths, and wore gloves. One caught hold of the bridle while two others centered their rifle sights on Fargo.

The fourth man came around, grabbed Fargo by the shirt, and hauled him from the saddle. He made no attempt to stop Fargo from falling, and chuckled when

Fargo thudded in the dirt. "Another cow for the slaughter."

"I thought it was lamb," one of the guards covering Fargo said.

"I thought it was lamb to the slaughter, not for the slaughter," said another.

"A cow is more fitting," the first guard said. Squatting, he gripped Fargo's chin. "My handle is Lester. I'll only say this once so listen close. You might have smallpox. We're going to keep you here until we know if you do or not."

Fargo had several questions he wanted to ask, but couldn't with the gag in his mouth. He grunted and worked his jaw but Lester did not take the hint.

"Make it easy on us and we'll be easy on you. Make it hard and you will damn well regret it. Once you are in the pen you are there to stay until we say different. Try to get away and we will shoot you dead. Any questions?" Lester grinned. "Oh. That's right. You can't say much, can you?"

"I'll open the gate," one of the others offered, and walked toward the shadowy structure.

Lester glanced at Fargo's feet. "They already took your boots? Usually they leave that for me." He nodded at the rest. "Lend a hand."

Fargo was dragged toward the pen. The silhouette resolved into a wooden fence fifteen feet high, resembling nothing so much as a gigantic corral. Only this corral held people, not livestock. At intervals enormous posts supported the rails. It would have taken twenty men a month of Sundays to build.

A huge gate was the only way in or out. Lester and the men with him hauled Fargo on through and flung him to the dirt like a sack of potatoes. When Fargo stopped rolling he was on his back staring at the stars.

"Remember what I told you and we'll get along," Lester said.

The gate creaked shut, their footsteps faded, and Fargo was left alone with the dark and the wind. Struggling onto his side, he tried to get some sense of how large the pen was. But the rest of the enclosure was as black as pitch. It was only here, near the gate, that the glow from the campfire reached.

An inky shape detached itself from the rest of the blackness and shuffled toward him. An old man, gray in the face as well as gray of hair, wearing scruffy clothes and socks but no shoes, came up and peered at him through narrowed eyes. "I don't know you." Turning, he melted into the blackness from whence he came.

Fargo was furious. The man had left him lying there, bound and gagged and helpless. He renewed his attempt to shed the gag but was thwarted. It seemed he was to be left there all night.

Then a second inky shape acquired substance. Much smaller than the old man, it had hair like corn silk. Fargo was not much of a judge of ages when it came to children, but he guessed she was ten to twelve years old. Her dress was as unkempt and dusty as the old man's shirt and pants had been. She was barefoot. "Who are you, mister?"

Fargo tried to answer but it was hopeless.

"What's the matter? Why can't you talk?" The girl inched nearer. Her small fingers brushed the bandanna. "Oh. They made it so you can't, is that it? That's too bad." Smiling, she, too, melted back into the blackness.

It wouldn't do Fargo any good to vent his spleen but he vented it anyway. He was fit to spit nails. Or split heads. His funk had about spent itself when the little girl returned with a larger image of herself. The adult version had the same corn silk hair and the same oval face, and was so thin she was a human beanpole. Her dress was as shabby as her daughter's. She, too, was barefoot. She showed no fear but came right up, and knelt.

"You were right to fetch me, Susie. This poor man needs our help." The woman pried at the knots in the bandanna and eventually succeeded in loosening them. With delicate care she pulled the other bandanna from his mouth. "There. Does that feel better?"

Fargo spat, then worked his jaw up and down and back

and forth. "I'm obliged," he said, his voice gruffer than he intended.

"I'm Calista Baxter. This imp beside me is my daughter, Susie."

"How long have you been here?" Fargo asked.

"Pretty near two months," Calista revealed.

"What?" Fargo assumed he had not heard correctly.

"Two months," the mother repeated. "The two worst months of my life. I've about given up any hope of ever leaving this pen."

"Why haven't they let you go? If you don't have smallpox by now, it should be safe to release you."

"It doesn't matter whether a person does or doesn't. Once someone is tossed in here, they never get out."

"Not ever?" Fargo was skeptical.

"They will keep you in here until you die."

10

Calista and Susie Baxter worked at the rope for long minutes. The knots defied them. Mother and daughter loosened a few, but the night riders had done a particularly thorough—some might say vicious—job. Some of the knots were like iron bubbles. The coils of rope were so tight they dug into Fargo's flesh.

"I'm sorry," the mother said. "We can't loosen some of these."

Fargo took a gamble. He had hesitated about mentioning the toothpick because he did not want anyone to know he had it. Twisting his neck, he verified the four guards were by the campfire. "Is that all of them?"

"Guards, you mean? Yes."

"Under my right pant leg," he said.

"I beg your pardon?"

"Look under my right pant leg. There should be a knife." Fargo could feel the sheath, but with all the bouncing and jouncing about he had done in the past couple of hours, he was not sure about the toothpick.

Acting slightly embarrassed, Calista slid her fingers up his pants. She groped a few seconds, said, "Oh!" and brought out her hand, her palm curled around the toothpick's hilt.

Fargo could have whooped for joy. "Start cutting," he directed. "Begin at the bottom and work your way up."

Calista complied. The toothpick was razor-sharp, but the rope was thick and it was soon obvious it would take her a while. At one point she said softly, "I'm sorry. I don't have much strength anymore. It's the lack of food and the strain."

"They don't feed you?"

"Once a day," Calista said. "At noon. But I haven't been getting my portion. If it wasn't for Susie sharing hers, I would have starved to death by now."

Fargo did not understand, and admitted as much. "Why don't you get your share? Do the guards refuse to give it to you?"

"Oh, no, it's not them," Calista said. "It's—" She abruptly stopped, and did not say more.

Little Susie was squatting at her mother's side. Every now and again she glanced over her shoulder into the veil of ink at the other end of the pen. She possessed exceptionally keen sight, because she suddenly gripped her mother's arm. "They're coming, Ma."

Intent on slicing yet another loop, Calista said without looking up, "Who is, dear?"

"Them." Fear filled the child's voice. She looked like a frightened rabbit ready to bolt.

The fear spread to the mother. "Dear God!" Calista's hand, and the toothpick, disappeared into the folds of her dress. When her hand reappeared, it was empty.

"What is going on?" Fargo asked. Their terror was unsettling.

Calista leaned so close, her lips brushed his ear. "If you value your life, don't mention your knife. Be careful what you say. Make them mad and they will kill you." She quickly rose and took a step back, her arm around Susie.

Two forms materialized out of the night. One was a man-mountain, a brutish block of muscle and bone with a shock of black hair and a ragged black beard. His hands were enormous, his fingers spikes, and his arms so long that his knuckles nearly scraped the ground when he walked. Beside him was a pint-sized image of himself. The same black hair, the same black beard, but as skinny as a rail and with the shifty features of a ferret.

"What do we have here?" rumbled the brutish mountain.

Calista, Fargo noticed, avoided meeting the newcomers' gazes. "The guards have thrown in a new one, Gront."

The block of muscle stared down at Fargo without a trace of friendliness. "Never saw you in Wet Grass, mister," he rumbled. "Who might you be?"

Fargo told them.

The skinny one bent until his nose practically touched Fargo's. He had dark, shifty eyes, and breath that reeked. "I don't think I like this one, brother. He might give us trouble."

Gront leaned on his huge fists and regarded Fargo with contempt. "He's puny, like the rest." Straightening, he said, "We're the Dross brothers, mister. I'm Gront. This here is Vole."

"How long have you been in here?" Fargo asked.

Gront's hairy face scrunched in thought. "I don't rightly recollect. From about when this whole thing began."

Fargo studied them. The stamp of hardship was not as severe on them as it had been on the old man, or on the mother and her child. They were not wasting away to nothing. Both were remarkably well fed and fit for two people who had been in the pen for so long.

"You a nosy bastard, is that it?" Vole growled. "It doesn't do to ask too many questions."

"I wish you wouldn't do that," Calista said quietly.

"Do what?"

"Swear in front of my daughter. I've asked you before not to, but you never listen."

Vole Dross jabbed a finger at her. "You don't ever tell us what to do. You hear me, woman?"

Calista meekly bowed her head. "I meant no disrespect. Gront knows that. Don't you, Gront?"

Before the walking mountain could answer, Vole grabbed Calista by the arm and shook her. "Damn your female hide! Cut that out! You don't think I see what you're up to, but I do."

"What is she up to, brother?" Gront asked.

"What she always is," Vole snapped. "She's trying to turn you against me. But she does it cleverlike."

Fargo thought he could distract them from her by saying, "I would be grateful if you would help me shed this rope."

"Who the hell cares what you want?" Vole snapped, still glaring at Calista. Suddenly shoving her, he spun on Fargo. "Let's get a few things straight, mister. My brother and me run things in here. Do as we tell you and we'll get along fine. Don't do as we tell you and the guards will haul your carcass out for the buzzards."

"Aren't we all in this together?"

Vole tittered and poked his hulking sibling. "You hear this idiot, Gront? He must be a Bible-thumper."

"Must be," the mountain rumbled. Then, leaning on one fist, Gront held the other close to Fargo's face. It was almost as big as Fargo's head. "See this? I can pound you to mush without half trying, so whatever you do, don't make me or my brother mad." He paused, and when Fargo did not say anything, he declared, "I mean it. If you don't believe me about the mush, ask anyone. I've done it before."

"You've killed some of those in quarantine?" Fargo did not hide his disgust. He had run into some scum in his travels, but these two were on a pinnacle all their own.

"Only the ones who gave us trouble," Gront said, as if that justified it.

"See that you don't," Vole warned. Nudging the Goliath, he wheeled. "Let's go back to sleep. This ain't worth our bother."

For perhaps two full minutes after they were gone no one said anything. Then Calista coughed. "Now you see how it is."

"Finish cutting me loose," Fargo instructed. "And while you're at it, tell me how you ended up in here." He watched in case the brothers returned.

Calista talked in a whisper. "It's been terrible. My husband and I have a farm east of Wet Grass. Or had, anyway. He died of smallpox. The evening after we buried him, the night riders showed up. They dragged Susie and me from our house and brought us to the pen. I begged them to let us go but they laughed in our faces."

She peered into the darkness. "The Dross brothers were already here."

Fargo waited.

"They say they were on their way to Oregon country. They were passing Wet Grass when they came on a man stumbling around in the dark. He had smallpox and died soon thereafter. They intended to ride on but the night riders showed up."

"How many others are in this pen?"

"Twenty-three. Five are men, the rest women and children. Women like me, who lost their husbands to the pox." Calista paused. "Seven people have died since I was brought here."

"From the disease?"

"No. At the hands of Gront and Vole." Calista trembled as she said it. "Anyone who stands up to them, they murder."

Fargo was incredulous. "The guards stand around and let it happen?"

"The guards don't care one whit about us. They would as soon we were all dead anyway."

"Are the guards settlers?"

"Heavens no. They work for Cole Narciss, and answer only to him. They are under his orders to shoot anyone who tries to escape. A settler named Pendergrast made it over the fence one night. But they tied a rope to his legs and dragged him around and around the pen until he died, so we could all see what is in store for us if we try the same thing."

"Does Narciss ever come by?" Fargo probed.

"Not once in all the months I've been here. No one does. Not a single living soul."

"But these people must have relatives and friends."

"Sure. But no one can come near us. We are under quarantine." Calista's eyes moistened. "No one is allowed within half a mile. Narciss has signs posted, warning that anyone who does will be shot on sight." She stopped cutting. "We are on our own, with no chance of ever leaving. Not this side of the grave, anyway."

"Ma," Susie suddenly whispered. "That other mean man is coming toward the gate."

Calista instantly whipped the Arkansas toothpick under her dress.

Fargo had been so intent on watching for the Dross brothers that he had not paid any attention to the guards.

The once called Lester had a rifle crooked in his elbow and suspicion on his countenance. "What are you doing there, Baxter?" he hollered.

"Untying Mr. Fargo, if that is all right," Calista said meekly.

"It didn't look like untying to me," Lester said. "Come over here, and be quick about it!"

The mother leaned toward her daughter. "Stay right where you are, no matter what he does. You promise?"

"Yes, Ma," Susie said, but she did not sound pleased.

Calista stood. As she rose, she moved her hand behind her and let go of the toothpick. It landed a few inches from Fargo's hand. Then, her head down, she went over to the gate.

"Turn around and hold your hands out from your sides," Lester ordered. Once she obeyed, he removed the bar and opened the gate wide enough to slip inside. Leering, he moved behind Calista and frisked her, patting and groping every inch of her body from her chin to her toes. In some parts he lingered more than others.

Deep scarlet flushed Calista's face. She silently endured the liberties he was taking, and when he was done, lowered her arms.

"I guess I was mistaken," Lester said. Chuckling, he backed out and closed and barred the gate. "Carry on with the untying. When you're done, shove the rope out or we'll come in and get it." He walked back to the fire.

Susie had tears in her eyes. She hugged her mother when Calista knelt and picked up the toothpick. "Oh, Ma," she said sadly. "I wish that awful man was dead. I wish all of them were dead."

"You shouldn't say things like that," Calista tenderly chided.

Fargo added Lester's name to the list he was compiling in his head. "I'm sorry you had to go through that on my account."

"Don't blame yourself," Calista said. "He does that several times a week. You were a convenient excuse."

"There is nothing you can do?"

"Who would I complain to? Narciss? He doesn't care what happens to us. I have no way of getting word to the other settlers, and even if I did, they are too scared to do anything about it." Calista shook her head. "No, I must deal with this on my own. I must do whatever it takes to keep my daughter and me alive." She resumed cutting the rope with one hand while pretending to tug at knots with the other.

Fargo was struck again by how weak and pale she was. He recalled her comment about the noon meal. "You never told me. Why don't you get to eat?"

"I'd rather not talk about it."

"Someone is taking your food? Is that it?"

Calista looked away. "Please. It is my problem. Not yours."

"You're cutting me free," Fargo said. "I figure I owe you."

"I don't want you hurt."

Little Susie put a hand on her mother's thin shoulder. "Tell him, Ma. I like this one. He's not like the others. Maybe he can help us."

"Hush, child."

"Tell him," Susie persisted. When her mother stayed silent, she whispered, "It's Gront. He takes her food for himself."

Something about Calista's expression spurred a suspicion in Fargo. "Just to fill his belly?"

"No." Calista shut her eyes and lowered her chin to her chest, and a single tear trickled from the corner of one eye. "He wants something from me. Until I give in, he won't let me eat."

Fargo did not ask what the "something" was. There was no need.

Smothering a sob, Calista said forlornly, "We are lost souls in a living hell, and there is nothing we can do about it."

"We'll see about that," Fargo said.

11

Fargo had never been one to turn the other cheek. When someone tried to punch his teeth in, he kicked theirs out. When someone tried to shoot him, he filled them with lead. It was well and good for those east of the Mississippi River to turn their cheeks if they wanted. The worst that ever happened to them was losing a purse to a footpad or running into a belligerent drunk. West of the Mississippi it was different. Thieves and drunks were common, but so were outlaws and hostiles and renegades of every stripe. Two-legged, rabid wolves who thought nothing of drawing their six-guns and shooting another person dead. They killed as casually as they drew breath. Anyone who turned the other cheek paid for their folly with their life.

But Fargo held his piece, and after what seemed half an eternity, the last of the rope coils parted and Fargo was free. He went to stand and regretted it when his body spiked with pain. His circulation had been cut off for so long that he could barely move his arms and legs. Lying on his back, he flexed and wriggled them in an attempt to restore movement. He felt the Arkansas toothpick slide into his ankle sheath, and said, "Thank you. I won't forget what you've done."

"Don't let anyone know you have the knife," Calista whispered. "Anyone caught with a weapon is beaten within an inch of their life."

"You don't have to stay with me if it will get you in trouble," Fargo said, thinking of the Dross brothers.

Calista divined his meaning. "Gront will be mad I helped you, but I doubt he'll lay a finger on me. Not out where everyone can see, anyway."

"Where do they make you sleep at night? On the ground?"

"Oh, no. They might like to, I suspect. But we have living quarters, such as they are. The guards will assign yours tomorrow." Calista paused, and smoothed the front of her dress. "You are welcome to spend the night with Susie and me. There is plenty of room."

"I would be happy to," Fargo said.

Calista smiled and began gathering the rope into a pile. "I'll take care of these, like Lester told us to."

"Wait." Fargo glanced at the campfire. The guards were sitting around drinking coffee. "If they see the rope has been cut, they'll know I have a knife." He could move a little. Sitting up, he took two pieces and tied the ends together.

"There will be an awful lot of knots," Calista mentioned.

Fargo shrugged. "I'll use small knots. Maybe they won't look too closely." He picked up another piece and tied it to the end. "Do the people in Wet Grass have any idea how all of you are being treated?"

"I am sure they don't," Calista said. "They are not permitted anywhere near here. The guards take turns going into the settlement. Once it was Lester's turn, and when he came back he bragged to me how he told everyone in the saloon how nice we have it. Three meals a day, shacks to live in, tubs for washing, that sort of thing."

Little Susie ran a hand through her stringy hair. "It's been so long since I took a bath, Ma, I've forgotten how."

A slow rage was building in Fargo, a rage the likes of which he had not felt in many a month. "They don't let you wash?"

Calista shook her head. "And we're only allowed a cup of water a day to drink. Some of us collect dew in

78

the morning using strips from our clothes. But there is never enough."

Fargo stopped tying knots and looked at her. "What's it all about? Why won't they let you leave? What is Narciss up to?"

"I have the same answer to all three questions," Calista said. "I simply don't know. I have tried and tried to make sense of it, but there isn't any rhyme or reason."

"There has to be an explanation," Fargo insisted. But it eluded him, whatever it was.

"When they first threw us in here," Calista related, "I was scared to death of coming down with smallpox. Not one of us has, yet those on the outside are still being afflicted. How can that be, when we're the ones who were exposed?"

"If I had the answer to that," Fargo speculated, "I might have the answer to everything."

"All I know," little Susie said, "is that I am always tired and hungry and dirty. I want to sleep without being afraid. I want to eat all I can eat. I want to wear clean clothes again."

Calista hugged her and pecked her on the head. "You will, dearest. I promise you that you will."

Soon Fargo had tied the last piece, bunched the rope up, and carried it to the gate. His legs were stiff and hurt terribly when he walked, but they pained him less the more he moved. He shoved the rope through a gap in the rails and was about to turn when the guard called Lester hollered.

"Hold up there, mister. I want a word with you."

Fargo did as he was told.

"Now that you're free, I don't want you getting any foolish notions," Lester lit right in. "I wasn't kidding earlier. We can make your life miserable if you don't behave."

"From what I hear, you've been doing a good job of making everyone miserable anyway."

Lester construed that as a compliment, and grinned. "Is that what she told you? Well, she should know. She's lasted longer than I would if I were in her place."

"You like frisking her, I noticed."

Lester's grin widened. "Wouldn't you? When she was first brought here she was as pretty as a sunset. She's on the scrawny side now, but she's still mighty easy on the eyes."

"I am going to enjoy this," Fargo said.

Again Lester misunderstood. "You're sleeping with her tonight? Hell, Gront will have a fit. He's been wanting to bed her for weeks."

"Is Gront a friend of yours?"

"That dumb ox? Neither he nor his brother are pards of mine," Lester answered, and added, "They're the same as the rest of you."

A peculiar thing to say, Fargo thought. It gave him more to ponder as Calista and Susie led him toward the far side of the pen. "How big is this place?"

"I'm not good at measures," Calista answered, "but I'd guess about sixty feet wide and a hundred feet long. A rectangle, you would call it. The wood came from the timber along the Platte. When Cole Narciss put his men to work building it, no one knew what to make of the thing. He wouldn't say what it was for. Some thought it might be for cows or horses, even though it's three times as high as any corral. Others figured maybe he was bringing in bulls to start a herd." She gazed about in open horror. "No one ever imagined it was for people."

Near the south end lean-tos had been erected. Calista ushered him into one. Up close, Fargo could see how poorly constructed it was, with gaps between the limbs. It was scant shelter from the sun or rain, and none whatsoever from the wind.

"This is what you live in?" Fargo had seen sturdier outhouses.

"Afraid so," Calista said. "Tomorrow or the next day some of the guards will go to the river and chop boughs for you to make your own."

Fargo found the information interesting. Hunkering, he discovered that the only items in the lean-to were two threadbare blankets. His rage climbed another notch. "These are all they give you?"

"It's not so bad right now, since it's summer," Calista said. "Once the cold weather hits, I doubt we will last long."

"You will be out of here long before then."

Calista cast worried glances to all sides, then whispered, "Don't talk like that! You can get in a lot of trouble."

"The guards can't hear me. They are too far off."

"I wasn't thinking of them," Calista said. She picked up one of the blankets and held it out. "You can have this if you want. I'll share Susie's."

Fargo refused to let his feelings show. But he made a secret vow. If it was the last thing he did, he would see to it that this woman and her child were set free. "You keep it. I can get by without one."

"Are you sure? It's awful chilly come daybreak. It sets my teeth to chattering sometimes."

It almost set Fargo's to chattering. He slept well enough until half an hour before dawn. The cold woke him. It wasn't that the temperature was anywhere near freezing. If he was to guess, he would say it dropped into the forties. Uncommonly low for that time of the year, and the brisk wind that tore through the lean-to made it seem colder. He curled into a ball and wrapped his arms around his legs, but his body warmth was not enough.

Calista and Susie were huddled close together and managed to sleep through until sunrise.

Fargo was one of the first up. To warm himself, he roamed among the lean-tos. It was like roaming through a graveyard of the living dead. Or the soon to be dead. The people were in bad shape, many worse off than Calista. Emaciated skeletons, surviving on will, their faces so thin and bony that they resembled hair-crowned skulls.

One lean-to, and its occupants, were exceptions. One lean-to was twice the size of any other. One-lean to was well constructed. The occupants were well fed. Both had several blankets, and, incredibly, pillows. Gront and Vole Dross were living like kings in a wasteland of paupers.

Fargo noticed something that gave him pause. Everyone else in the pen, as near as he could tell, was barefoot.

But not the Dross brothers. They were allowed the luxury of shoes. Good pairs of store-bought shoes. It lent more substance to his suspicion.

The eastern horizon gave birth to a rosy glow as Fargo walked to the north end of the pen. Three of the guards were asleep near the fire, bundled in blankets. The fourth was supposed to be keeping watch. He was sitting up, but his chin was on his chest and he snored lightly.

Fargo was tempted to make his bid then and there. But just then the guard on duty snapped awake with a start, yawned, and looked about him. It was Lester. He spotted Fargo. Anger animating him, he came over to the gate.

"What the hell are you doing?"

"Admiring the accommodations," Fargo answered.

"You're not allowed near this end of the pen unless we call you over," Lester growled. "Next time, I'll put a window in your noggin."

"Calista mentioned something about cutting wood for my lean-to," Fargo remarked.

"We'll get around to it when I'm good and ready," Lester said. "Until then you can sleep in the open."

"You like lording it over these people, don't you?"

Lester gripped the bar that held the gate closed but did not lift it. "Watch that mouth, mister. You're in over your head here. Better start treating me with respect or you won't last long."

"By respect you mean lick your boots?" Fargo said.

Lester did not become madder. Instead, he laughed in sadistic delight. "Call it what you want. But sure I like it. I hold the life of everybody here in the palm of my hand. All I have to do is squeeze to snuff a wick."

"Are you in charge of the other guards?"

"Smart boy," Lester taunted.

"Are you in charge of the Dross brothers, too? Or are they over you?"

Lester's dark eyes narrowed and his mouth became a tight slit. "Maybe too damn smart. Not that it will do you any good. You're going to die in here. You will slowly rot away and in a few months we will bury you, and if the law or anyone ever comes around looking for you, we'll tell them it was the smallpox."

"And if they dig me up, they won't find any bullet holes," Fargo said. "Mighty convenient, that smallpox."

Lester's smile was vicious. "Ain't it, though? Now suppose you mosey on back to where you belong before I shoot you anyway."

Fargo's suspicion was now a conviction. He retraced his steps. A golden ring was visible to the east. Spreading sunlight glistened in the dew that speckled the grass. Near the pen it glistened brighter than elsewhere. Bright pinpoints of light, many scores of them, like earthbound fireflies. Fargo had never witnessed anything quite like it. He drifted toward the east side of the fence. The fireflies, he saw, were in a strip about five yards wide that bordered the pen.

It was glass.

Broken shards and pieces, thousands of them. Fragments of labels told Fargo where the glass came from: liquor bottles. Empties from the saloon, no doubt collected and brought out once every couple of weeks. No wonder everyone, or nearly everyone, was made to go barefoot. If they made it over the fence without being shot, they would rip their feet open trying to cross the glass.

Fargo had not noticed if glass had been scattered near the gate. He would make it a point to find out.

Calista was awake. She lay on her back, Susie's head cradled in her arm, and smiled. "There you are. I was worried. I was about to come looking for you."

"I could go for a dozen eggs right about now," Fargo mentioned. "With bacon and toast and half a pot of coffee."

A pained expression came over her. "Don't mention food, please. I can't bear to think of it or my stomach hurts. I would give anything for a good meal."

Fargo sank down, cross-legged. "Soon you can have all the food you want."

"What are you talking about?"

"You won't be in this hellhole must longer," Fargo

told her. "I'm leaving and I'm taking you with me. You, and anyone else who wants to go."

"You're forgetting the guards. They'll have a thing or two to say about that."

Fargo gazed toward the campfire. "Dead men can't say anything."

Calista gave him a strange look. "I almost believe you. But others have tried and gotten nowhere. It's always the same. When people are thrown in here, they want out right away. But as time goes by and they realize there is no escape, all the spirit goes out of them. They become like everyone else. Waiting around to die."

"I never was fond of twiddling my thumbs," Fargo said.

12

Cadavers came to life and shambled about the pen. Their cold veins needed the warmth of the sun.

None showed any interest in Fargo. They moved woodenly, their faces lifeless masks. A pall of despair and misery hung over them like a cloud.

Fargo walked with Calista and Susie. The girl flapped her thin arms, and now and then hopped up and down, but she kept shivering and saying, "I'm freezing, Ma."

"It wouldn't be so bad if they fed us breakfast," Calista said.

The last to emerge from their lean-to were the Dross brothers. Fargo had been watching for them, and he saw the huge Gront unfurl, stretch, and pat his gut. Vole stepped out after him and poked his brother, saying something that made Gront look sheepish.

Inwardly, Fargo smiled grimly to himself. Outwardly, he asked, "How many of these people would fight to break out of here?"

"Once I would have said all of them," Calista answered. "Now, most are wasted to near ruin. A few might be willing, but they are too weak to be of much use, me included."

"I'll go it alone, then," Fargo said.

Calista placed a hand on his arm. "I can't begin to guess what you have in mind, but you are only one man. You will be killed."

Fargo did not comment.

"There is glass spread outside the pen," Calista said,

"so even if you made it over the fence, your feet would be cut to ribbons before you got very far."

"I know about the glass."

"Do you know that some of the rails have been cut partway through on the outside so that if you were to climb them they would break under your weight? Do you know that long nails have been pounded through many of the rails so the sharp ends stick out? Do you know that other rails have rope strung along them, and that if the rope is jarred, even a little, it sets a bell to ringing out at the gate?"

Fargo admitted he had not known any of that.

"They think of everything," Calista said bitterly. "Or should I say Cole Narciss does? He's a fiend, that one."

"All this to keep smallpox from being spread," Fargo said. "Didn't it make you wonder?"

"I'm not sure I understand. Smallpox is nothing to trifle with. It could wipe out the entire settlement."

Fargo had several questions he wanted to ask but a giant shadow fell across them. Susie bleated like a lamb and threw herself into her mother's arms.

Gront Dross had his big hands on his big hips. His attitude was that of a bear in a mean mood. "You're the new one. Remember what I told you? My brother and me run things. If we say to jump, you ask how high."

From behind the hulking mountain stepped Vole Dross. His sneer seemed carved in place, but it wavered a bit when he raked Fargo up and down with a close scrutiny. "You're taller than you looked last night. And you've got more muscles than most."

"Not more than me," Gront bragged.

"No one has more than you," Vole said. "Maybe we should give this new one some work so the others will see he's no different than anyone else."

"Whatever you want, Vole," Gront said. "You're the smart one. What should we have him do?"

Fargo was amused by how they talked about him as if he were not there. He folded his arms across his chest and shifted so his left side was toward them.

"Please," Calista interjected. "He's new, like you said. Can't you leave him be?"

"Stupid woman," Vole said. "It's the new ones who have to be put in their place so they don't get any wild notions."

"No sass allowed," Gront said, and spread his enormous arms wide. "Or they have me to deal with."

Vole gazed about the pen. "I have it!" he exclaimed. "How about if we have him clean all the lean-tos? Except ours. He can shake out the blankets, tidy them up, that sort of thing."

"Like a maid, you mean," Gront rumbled, and laughed. "I like it. If he does a good job, he can be the maid permanent."

Vole motioned. "What are you waiting for, mister? You heard us. Get to work. When you're done we'll have something else for you to do."

"I have a better idea," Fargo said. "Why don't you two clean the lean-tos? And while your at it, pick the one you want to sleep in from now on."

Gront thought that was hilarious. "We already have one, stupid. It's better than any of the others. We're not about to swap."

"It was yours. It's mine now."

Amazement delayed their response. They looked at one another, then at Fargo, then at one another again. "Your joke's not so funny," Vole said.

Sidling to the right so Calista and Susie would not be near him when the explosion came, Fargo asked, "Why did Narciss pick the two of you? Because you're good at scaring women and children? It sure wasn't for your brains."

"Hey, now," Vole Dross snarled, and swore.

His outburst caused many of the walking cadavers to stop and turn. Those nearest instinctively started to back away.

"When did Narciss hire you?" Fargo asked. "Before he came west? Does it go that far back? Or was that story of yours about being bound for Oregon true and he hired you in Wet Grass?"

Gront's mouth dropped open and his jaw worked a few times before he got anything out. "He knows, Vole! Somehow he knows!"

"Shut up, you simpleton!" Vole shouted. "He doesn't know a damn thing! He's trying to trick us, but we won't let him." He looked up at his colossal sibling. "Kill him, brother. Kill him quick."

Gront Dross instantly lunged, seeking to enfold Fargo in a bear hug. The outcome was foreordained. No one could hope to break the man-mountain's grip. Gront's arms were tree trunks bulging with corded sinew.

Fargo knew he could not match Gront's brute strength. But he did not have to, so long as his agility and quickness did not fail him. Gront was a bear to his wolf, and like a wolf, he nimbly ducked and sprang aside before Gront's arms closed.

Stepping in close, Fargo flicked several swift punches to Gront's ribs. It was like punching an anvil. Fargo accomplished little other than to hurt his hands. He leaped back and crouched.

Gront was surprised. Unaffected by the blows, he complained to his brother, "This one hops around like a damn rabbit."

"So what?" Vole shot back. "Keep after him. Never let up. You'll wear him down just like you wear them all down. He doesn't stand a chance."

"He sure doesn't," Gront said, and laughed smugly. "How do you want me to do it when I catch him? Crush his chest or break his back?"

"Why not do both?" Vole suggested.

Gront laughed some more. "I'll mangle him to a pulp, and Lester can feed the remains to the turkey buzzards and the coyotes."

"Now you're talking," Vole said. "Bust him bad! Spill the bastard's blood!"

Fargo was coiled and waiting. He must not let their chatter distract him. He must stay focused on Gront and only Gront so when—

Voicing a guttural growl, the titan attacked. He moved

faster this time, but still not fast enough. Fargo evaded a blow that would have caved in his face had it landed.

"Stop hopping around, damn you!" Gront bellowed. "You're only making me mad, and the madder I get, the worse it will be for you."

Fargo stood still, his hands at his sides. "I wouldn't want that," he replied. "Make it quick so I don't suffer."

Elated, Gront grinned and opened his arms wide for another bear hug. Too late, he heard his brother shout a warning.

"It's a trick, you damned yack!"

Fargo started his swing down near the ground. He hit the bigger man squarely on the chin and rocked Gront on his heels.

Rubbing his jaw, Gront said in genuine admiration, "That's some right arm you have there. In all my born days I've never been hit so hard. I felt it clear down to my toes."

Fargo stared at his fist. Usually when he slugged someone they went down and stayed down.

"That's some arm," Gront repeated. "But it's not enough. I've never been beat. Not ever." He was not boasting. He was stating fact.

"There's a first time for everything," Fargo said. Careful to stay out of reach, he slowly circled, seeking an opening.

"Not when I have my brother on my side," Gront said. "He's sneaky. He knows just when to slow them down."

The next moment a pair of strong arms wrapped tight around Fargo's legs. He had forgotten to keep an eye on Vole.

"I've got him, brother! Bring him down!" Vole whooped. "Bring him down and break his bones!"

Fargo sought to kick Vole away but the runt clung on. He slammed a punch at Vole's head only to have the ferret twist so he only landed a glancing blow. Fargo snapped back his arm to swing again—and a ten-ton boulder smashed into his chest and slammed him to the ground. His lungs emptied in an excruciating *whoosh*, and before he could suck in more air, fingers as thick as sledge handles clamped onto his neck.

Gront grinned like a cat who had just caught a canary. Vaguely, Fargo was aware that Vole had let go of his legs. "I've got you now!" the living mountain crowed. "I've got you and there's no escape!" His sinews bulged. "I'm going to squeeze your neck from your shoulders like I used to do with chickens when I was little."

Fargo clawed at Gront's fingers but it was like clawing at iron bands. They dug inexorably into his throat.

"You're doing it, brother!" Vole Dross shrieked for joy. "He's starting to turn purple!"

Dimly, Fargo heard Calista call his name. There was a commotion of some sort but he could not spare the seconds to find out what caused it. His chest was molten fire, and his vision was blurring. He placed his hands on Gront's face and pushed.

The colossus chortled. "You'll have to do better than that, mister. A whole lot better."

Fargo thought so, too. He dug his thumbs into Gront's eyes and gouged using all his strength, slicing with the hard edges of his fingernails.

Yowling like a gut-shot mongrel, Gront heaved back onto his knees and covered his bleeding eyes. "He's blinded me, Vole!" he bawled. "I can't see nothing but red!"

"Let me look!" Vole tried to pull his brother's huge hands off. "Let me see what he did!"

For the moment Fargo was forgotten. Gasping for breath, he scrambled backward, onto his hands and knees. Vole had his back to him and Gront had his eyes closed.

Fargo reached for the Arkansas toothpick. Sluggish from nearly having the life choked out of him, he was slow to realize that a guard had hold of Calista, and had a hand clamped over her mouth. She was looking right at him, or rather, past him, and her eyes were wide in horror.

Fargo tried to turn but he was only halfway around when he glimpsed Lester. A hardwood rifle stock demonstrated why it was superior to the human skull. The world burst apart in a shower of white lights that gradually faded to near black. He was still conscious, but barely. Hands slid under his arms. He was dragged facedown. Suddenly one of the men dragging him yipped in alarm.

"Look out! What's he doing?"

A tree fell on Fargo's shoulders. He was mashed flat. Clubs rained down. Belatedly, he realized they were not clubs, but fists. Huge fists. Gront Dross's fists. In Gront's rage, more of his blows struck Fargo's shoulders than his head.

Sounds of a struggle ensued. Amazingly, someone was trying to stop him. "Enough, damn you!" Lester rasped. "You're killing him!"

The blow stopped. "Do you see my eyes?" Gront roared. "Do you see what he did to them?"

"They're scratched, is all," Lester replied. "You can still see."

"I want him to hurt!"

"Then do it my way," Lester said. "He'll beg to be put out of his misery before I'm done."

"You promise?"

"Remember that drummer I staked out over an anthill?"

Gront's weight lifted. "We'll do it your way. But you better come up with something good."

Over the next several minutes Fargo would black out, snap back to consciousness, and black out again. He must have done it six or seven times. When at last he opened his eyes and they stayed open, he winced at new pain in his wrists and ankles. Confusion set in. He blinked, seeking to understand why the ground and the sky had changed places. Then it hit him. He was upside down.

They had tied him to the pen fence.

Gront and Vole were smirking. Lester and the rest of the guards wore gleeful grins. Well back, afraid to come closer, were Calista and Susie and the rest of the quarantined scarecrows.

"How long, do you reckon?" Lester asked, poking a bony finger at Fargo. "How long can you last?"

Nausea nipped at Fargo, preventing him from answering. He felt light-headed, almost dizzy.

Cupping a hand to an ear, Lester said, "I can't hear you." He and his friends cackled. "Maybe you think you can pull one over on us. Maybe you think you can cut yourself free or have one of these wretches do it."

The Dross brothers and the other guards laughed louder.

Lester's left hand came into view. He was holding the Arkansas toothpick. "Think again."

13

Agony such as Fargo had seldom suffered. The pain, the throbbing pain in his wrists and ankles and head, the awful ache in his chest that grew worse as the hours went by. The heat, the searing, burning heat that grew hotter as the sun rose higher and the temperature inexorably climbed.

Fargo's thirst was terrible. His throat was parched, his mouth desert-dry. Sweat poured from him in great drops until there was barely any moisture left in his body. He craved water, craved it more than anything. His lips were puffy and split, but he had no spit with which to moisten them.

Lester and the other guards stuck around for a while, taunting and laughing. But they soon tired of their sport and left the pen.

The Dross brothers had a perfect chance to beat on him, to inflict as much torment as they wanted, but they drifted off to their lean-to.

As for the rest of the pen's cadaverous denizens, most stayed well away from the part of the fence where Fargo hung. Lester had warned them that anyone inclined to help him would pay, and pay dearly, and the threat was heeded. Some came near and stared sadly, notably Calista and little Susie.

Fargo did not blame them. If there was any blame it was his own. He had been careless and overconfident, and it had cost him. He should have waited until dark to brace the Dross brothers, and done it quietly so the guards were not alerted.

Stupid, stupid, stupid, Fargo thought, and tried to ignore the hideous thirst that ate at him like acid. What he wouldn't give for a sip of water. A single sip. He had lost track of how many hours he had hung there. It was past noon, he knew that much. About two or three, based on the sun.

Calista and Susie were still there, staring.

Fargo tried to smile but his mouth would not work as it should. The best he could manage was a grimace.

Calista glanced about her, then started to come toward him. She was saying something, saying it so softly that Fargo could not hear her. He tried to warn her to stay back but all that came out was a croaked, "Don't—"

Suddenly Susie gripped her mother's arm and pointed.

Calista promptly scooped the girl into her arms and made off across the enclosure.

Her reason was twofold: the Dross brothers. Huge Dross and small Dross swaggered up and stood, chuckling and grinning.

"What do we have here, brother?" Vole said. "Someone must have stuck it up to scare off the birds."

Gront rumbled with mirth. "That was a good one, brother. Speaking of birds"—and he craned his thick neck back to regard the sky—"I don't see any buzzards yet, but give them a day or two and they'll come to feast. They always do."

"Once he's ripe enough for them," Vole said. "We should cut him down and stake him out on the plain, then sit on the top rail and watch."

"That would be fun," Gront agreed. "I always like it when the buzzards rip out the innards. Those long ropes we've got inside. What are they called again?"

"Intestines."

"That's them. The buzzards always get to fighting over the intestines. They have regulars tugs of war."

"I like it when they go for the eyes," Vole said. "Their big beaks dig into the sockets and out the eyeballs pop, like peas from a pod."

Fargo tried to ignore them but his self-control was not what it should be. "Bastards," he rasped.

"Listen!" Vole exclaimed. "He can still speak!"

"It's a wonderment!" Gront declared. "But it's good he's using his tongue while he still has one. Buzzards are fond of them, as I recollect." Stepping closer, he balled a fist and drew back his arm, but after a few moments he lowered it without striking. "No. I might bust you up inside and you'd die, and we don't want that. Not yet. Not for a good, long while."

"Ever heard of the Apaches?" Vole asked Fargo. "Folks say they can torture better than anyone. But those folks haven't seen my brother and me. We'll let you hang another couple of days, then set to work. You'll scream until your lungs are fit to burst. After we're done, we'll stake you out for the buzzard and coyotes."

All Fargo could do was glare. But his trigger finger twitched, and went on twitching.

"Tell you what," Gront said to his small imitation. "Let's go have a drink. All the nice, cool water we want."

Startled, Vole looked right and left and then jabbed his brother none too gently. "Keep your voice down, you simpleton. Do you want everyone to hear you?"

"They'll think we're only funning," Gront answered.

"Some might not. A few are beginning to suspect," Vole said. "The boss will be mad if they find out."

"So what?" Gront gestured at several shuffling scarecrows. "Look at them. They're sheep. There's not a damn thing they can do."

"If he says not to let them know, then we damn well better not," Vole insisted. "He's a hellion when he's mad."

"I'm not scared of him," Gront said.

"I'm not scared of rattlers, either, but that doesn't mean I want one to bite me. Make no mistake, brother. He's snake-mean, that one. He'd shoot us as soon as look at us if we don't do exactly as he says."

"You fret too much," was Gront's opinion.

"You don't fret enough."

They took their argument, and themselves, off to their lean-to, leaving Fargo to contemplate what he would like to do if he could somehow free himself, and who he would like to do it to.

The afternoon waned. The heat became almost unbearable. The pain was slightly easier to endure, but only because Fargo became used to it. Still, it dulled his senses and gnawed at his will until along about twilight, when he succumbed.

Tugging on his wrist brought Fargo back to life. He opened his eyes. It was pitch black, so black that for a few moments he thought someone had placed a blindfold over his eyes or something was affecting his vision. Then he saw stars far above, and shadowy shapes next to him. "You shouldn't."

"Hush," Calista said, prying furiously at a rope.

"If they catch you—" Fargo did not finish. Susie was trying to free his other arm.

"We don't care," Calista whispered. "We will free you if it takes all night." She hissed in frustration. "But these knots are so tight! If only we had that knife of yours."

Fargo licked his cracked lips. To his surprise, he had enough saliva to do it. "Can you reach between the bottom rails?"

"Sure. But why?"

"The glass they've scattered. Find a piece big enough and sharp enough," Fargo instructed.

Calista was moving before he stopped talking. Kneeling, she extended her left arm and gingerly felt about. She found a piece, examined it, and said, "This won't do." She groped for another.

The pen lay quiet and still under the canopy of darkness, but Fargo was deathly worried for the mother and her child. At any moment the Dross brothers or a guard might notice them.

"This one won't do, either."

"Want me to help, Ma?"

"No. You could cut yourself." Calista inspected and discarded half a dozen pieces without finding one that suited her.

"I think I hear someone," Susie whispered.

Both froze.

Fargo had heard it, too. It could have been the wind, or the scrape of a sole. He listened, scarcely breathing.

At length, apparently satisfied it had been nothing of consequence, Calista resumed picking through the glass. She was becoming impatient and groped with less care. Suddenly her arm jerked, and she let loose a low "Ouch." Then, to Fargo, she whispered, "Sorry. Cut myself."

"Any sharp piece will do," Fargo suggested.

"They're too small," Calista replied. "It would take forever to cut through the ropes." Even as she said it, she examined yet another piece and remarked, "I guess I spoke too soon."

Fargo's eyes were sufficiently adjusted to the dark for him to see that the piece she held was from the bottom of a large liquor bottle. In the shape of a scythe, it was over five inches long. The upper third was thinner and as sharp as a saber. The edges to the lower part were dull, making for a suitable handle.

Without delay Calista began cutting. She freed his wrists first, then stretched to reach his ankles.

"Let me." Fargo took the piece of glass. He had to try three times before he levered his body high enough to grip the rail his ankles were tied to. Once that was accomplished, he swiftly sliced through the last ropes. As the final strands parted, he gripped a rail so he would not drop like a rock.

Fargo was free but he hurt like hell. He slowly straightened. His arms and legs throbbed. Some of the pain was the result of cramps. Flexing his limbs helped a little. He held onto the piece of glass.

"What now?" Calista whispered. "There is nowhere you can hide that they can't find you."

Scaling the fence was out of the question. Fargo might make it over, but he would be no better off out on the prairie unless he had a horse and weapons. Besides, he never liked to tuck tail and run if there was a better way. "Go to your lean-to. Stay there until I say it is safe."

"What about you?"

"I feel like a stroll." Fargo watched until they blended into the night, then he crouched and stalked toward the large lean-to. From others he passed came a variety of snores. From one came whimpering and sobs.

The loudest snoring, appropriately enough, came from the largest source. Gront and Dross were a few feet apart, Gront on the outside of the lean-to. Their heads were at opposite ends, which struck Fargo as strange, making it easier for him.

Gront was on his back, an enormous arm across his chest, the other beside him. His mouth moved as he snored. His head was back, his neck covered by his bushy beard. The hair brushed Fargo's hand as he placed the edge of the glass against the left side of Gront's throat. Gront did not wake up.

Fargo thought of what the brothers had done to him. He thought of what they had done to Calista. He sliced the glass as deep as it would go and slit Gront's throat from from ear to ear.

Gront went on snoring, but not for long. Sputtering and gurgling, he abruptly sat up. His hand flew to his throat and he bleated in fear. He looked wildly about, and saw Fargo.

"Remember me?"

Gront Dross made a vain effort to stanch the flow. But as big as his hands were, as powerful as his fingers were, blood sprayed in a fine mist. He tried to say something, but the only sound he made, the last sound he was to ever utter, was a wet slobbery mew that ended with his enormous bulk collapsing, never to move again.

Fargo wiped the glass dry on Gront's shirt, then glided to the other end of the lean-to.

Vole Dross was not snoring but he was deep in dreamland. Vole's ferret features twitched but otherwise he did not stir when Fargo squatted and held the bloody tip of the piece of glass over Vole's right eye. With his other hand Fargo tapped Vole's cheek. At the fourth tap Vole's eyes shot open, and the instant they did, Fargo thrust the glass into the right socket as deep as it would go. At the same time, he shifted and slammed his knee onto Vole's chest to hold him down while clamping his hand over Vole's mouth.

The eruption was brief. The smaller Dross bucked and sputtered and hissed, and died.

Fargo sat with his back to the lean-to and wiped his hands on Vole's shirt. He was suddenly tired. Weary to his core. But he had more to do. A lot more. First he dragged Vole's body from the lean-to. He began to drag Gront, but it was like trying to drag a steam engine. He rolled the body out.

Fargo went through their pockets. Gront's yielded ten dollars in coins and a rusty folding knife. That was all. Vole, though, turned out to be more pack rat than ferret. His pockets contained twenty-four dollars, a pair of dice, a deck of cards, a tobacco pouch, lucifers, a piece of jerky, and a sheet of paper.

Fargo unfolded it. It was a note, scrawled in ink. Holding the paper so it caught what little starlight there was, he bent close.

Gentlemen,
   If the terms I have offered are acceptable, be in Wet Grass by the end of the month. You will be paid when the job is done.

That was all. It was not signed.

Fargo went through their bedding but did not find what he was certain was there. He shoved the blankets and pillows from under the lean-to and did what to others might seem peculiar; he smacked the ground, starting at one end and working toward the other. Midway the sound was different. Opening the rusty folding knife, he scraped at the dirt, uncovering several boards about a foot and a half long. The boards covered a hole.

The cache consisted of a water skin, a half-eaten loaf of bread, Saratoga chips, enough jerky to feed an army, and more. But the item that excited Fargo the most was one he had not expected to find: a loaded derringer. He pocked it, then lifted the water skin out.

The skin was wonderfully cool to the touch. The slosh of the water inside caused his throat to constrict in anticipation. Carefully opening it, he sipped. Never, in all his life, had water tasted so delicious.

Fargo leaned back against a pole. There was no hurry. Plenty of time until dawn. He drank slowly, sparingly, in order not to become sick. Between swallows he chewed a piece of jerky. Gradually, newfound vigor seeped into his body. The pain lessened.

But just when things were finally going his way, the night disgorged two surprises in the forms of two men stalking toward him.

14

In a twinkling the derringer was in Fargo's hand and he reared from under the lean-to. The two men stopped. Only then did Fargo note how thin they were, and their ghastly complexions.

"Don't shoot!" one cried, but not too loudly, so as not to be heard out by the gate. "It's Rob Howard and Edgar Rice from Wet Grass. We want to talk to you."

Fargo did not lower the derringer. Not once since he had been thrown into quarantine had the two men spoken to him. Now all of a sudden they wanted to. "Come closer," he commanded.

Acting nervous, they did, and when they were six feet away, Fargo said, "That's far enough. Say your piece."

"We want to help you," the man who had identified himself as Rob Howard said. "We were awake. We saw Calista free you."

"We kept it to ourselves," Edgar Rice said, as if that were something to be proud of. He was older, a bundle of bones in ragged clothes.

"But you didn't help her."

"We've been in here a lot longer than you," Edgar Rice said. "Look at us. I'm so weak I can barely stand. Rob, here, isn't much better off. Another couple of weeks and we'll be worm food."

"You say that you are from Wet Grass?" Fargo prodded.

Edgar Rice nodded. "I owned the general store. Rob owned the saloon. The night riders came for us. Claimed we had been exposed to smallpox." He swore angrily. "We wound up in this damnable pen."

"I was told that Cole Narciss owns the saloon and the general store," Fargo said.

"Not legally, he doesn't," Edgar Rice replied. "After we were quarantined Narciss took them over. He never offered to buy them—never paid Rob or me a cent. Yet now he tells everyone they're his."

"Has he laid claim to other properties?"

"All the people in here own property," Rob Howard answered. "All of them have lost their property to Cole Narciss."

"You don't say," Fargo said. The whole affair had taken on new significance. There was more behind the quarantine than preventing the spread of smallpox. No wonder Calista and the others had been held for so long. Narciss had a secret motive.

"Give that polecat another six months," Edgar Rice said, "and he'll own Wet Grass lock, stock, and barrel."

"Fetch the rest," Fargo directed.

"I beg your pardon?" asked Edgar.

"Wake them up. Have them gather around. I want you to tell them the same thing you just told me."

Rob Howard fidgeted. "But they're all asleep. Can't it wait until sunrise?"

"And have Lester and his pards wonder what we're up to?" Fargo shook his head. "If you two want out of here, if you want your businesses back, if you have a hankering to pay Cole Narciss back for all the suffering he caused you, then fetch the rest, and do it now." He had persuaded them. As they hastened away, he added, "Do it quietly, too."

It took half an hour. Some came quickly. Others, weaker or more timid, dragged their heels. They sat in a silent half circle in front of the large lean-to, the ravages they had endured seared into their sepulchral faces.

They were people at the end of their rope, and Fargo was about to throw them a new one. He passed around the water skin, making sure no one drank more than a few mouthfuls. He gave each person a handful of jerky to start, with the promise of more to follow. Their amazement eclipsed the fear many had shown at sight of the bodies.

Then, cross-legged under the lean-to, Fargo began. "Many of you are wondering what this is about. Many of you are wondering where the water and the food came from." He pointed at the Dross brothers. "Didn't any of you wonder why those two stayed well fed while the rest of you starved? Didn't it seem strange to you that they could kill and get away with it? That they were on such friendly terms with the guards?" He paused to let that sink in. "Gront and Vole weren't under quarantine like the rest of you. They were planted in the pen to keep you in line. Lester saw to it they had all the food and water they needed. They kept it hidden in a hole under their blankets."

"God in heaven," someone said, aghast.

"Cole Narciss is using the smallpox as an excuse to take over Wet Grass," Fargo said. He explained about the confiscated property. "The question is, are you willing to let him get away with it?"

They weren't. Murmurs of anger and resentment leaped from throat to throat until Fargo worried they were making too much noise and silenced them.

"I feel the same way as you. I don't have any land at stake. Just my pride," Fargo said grimly. "The sons of bitches who did this to me have a reckoning coming."

"What do we do, mister?" Edgar Rice asked. "We're not in any shape for a fight. But we'll help any way we can."

They drank more water and ate more food, and while they drank and ate, Fargo told them the part they were to play. They listened in rapt attention, new life in their expressions, new gleams in their eyes. He ended with, "The sooner we do it, the more miles we can put behind us by dawn."

Rob Howard stood. "I think I speak for all of us when I say we are as ready right this second as we will ever be."

Calista also rose. "Don't forget the children. Two of

the women should take them over by the south fence and have them lie on the ground with their backs to the lean-tos, then make sure they close their eyes and stick their fingers in their ears."

"But I want to stay with you, Ma," Susie protested.

Gently squeezing her daughter's arm, Calista said, "There are some things children your age should not see."

Fargo slowly stood. "Let's do it."

Lester happened to be sitting by the fire. The rest of the guards were under their blankets. He was poking a stick at a few stray embers and did not hear Calista come to the gate. He jumped when she called his name. "Damn, woman! You shouldn't sneak up on a man like that."

"I didn't mean to," Calista said contritely.

Lester dropped the stick, picked up his rifle, and warily approached. "What are you doing over here at this time of night, anyhow? You should be asleep."

"I thought you should know."

"Know what?" Lester snapped. He rose on the tips of his boots to peer past her, and stiffened. "What is that light yonder?"

"A fire," Calista said.

Lester reached the gate in several long bounds. "The hell you say! Who made it? I'll rip their lungs out."

"That's why I'm here," Calista continued to play her part. "It's those two brothers, Gront and Vole. They're drunk."

"What?"

"They got hold of a bottle somewhere and have been drinking since sunset," Calista said. "I'm surprised you didn't hear them, with all the joking and laughing they've been doing. A while ago Vole complained that it was getting brisk so they built a small fire."

"The hell you say!" Lester heaped swear words on the Drosses. Then he barked at Calista to step back, and raised the bar. "They think they can do any damn thing they please, do they? Well, they have another think coming! They are under orders, the same as me."

"Sorry?" Calista said.

"Nothing." Lester turned and bellowed at his sleeping companions, who spilled from under their blankets in a befuddled state.

"What is it, Les?" one wanted to know. "What is all the fuss?"

"It's those lunkheads, Gront and Vole," Lester replied. "They're having a private revel without the proper say-so." He waggled his rifle. "Which one of you idiots gave them a bottle?"

The three men looked at one another. Each denied being the culprit.

"Well, they got the damn bottle *somewhere*," Lester snarled. They entered the pen and he pulled the gate shut. Then, taking Calista by the arm, Lester pushed her toward the flames dancing in the dark. "There will be hell to pay for this. Just see if there isn't."

"I sure wouldn't want to be in their boots when you know who finds out," another guard remarked.

In the light of the fire the huge form of Gront Dross could be seen leaning against one of the support poles. Vole was under a blanket, his head cushioned on a pillow.

"Look at those jackasses," Lester fumed. "No one is going to believe they were put in here under quarantine like everyone else."

"Gront never was very smart," a third man commented. "But if you tell him I said that, I'll brand you a liar."

Fargo heard it all. He was on his belly under a blanket in the shadow of another lean-to. As the foursome marched past, he rose and, leaving the blanket bundled at his feet, crept after them. He was not the only one. From other points rose other hidden figures who stalked toward the quartet. Walking corpses out for revenge on those responsible for their condition.

Without breaking stride, Lester suddenly shoved Calista so hard that she stumbled and fell. He walked on past her, his voice a bullwhip. "Gront! Vole! What in hell do you two think you are playing at?" When neither

105

answered, he shook a fist. "Answer me, damn it! I've had all of this nonsense I am going to abide!"

Fargo moved faster. He was almost to the last of the four, who had fallen slightly behind the others.

"Gront! You hear me?" Lester fumed. "Just because you're as big as a bull doesn't give you the right to do as you damn well please. We are all in this together."

"Something ain't right," a guard at Lester's elbow said.

Lester halted, apparently realizing the same thing. "Vole? Why doesn't your brother answer?"

By then Fargo was only a step from the last man. He had hoped to take them by surprise but, as he sprang, the guard next to Lester glanced right and left and bawled, "Look! It's the whole bunch of them!"

"It's a trap!" the fourth man bleated.

As all four guards snapped their rifles to their shoulders, Fargo jammed the derringer against the temple of the last man and fired. He immediately sprang for the next. The derringer held two shots.

Rifles boomed, and scarecrows dropped. But the rest of the captives kept coming.

The third guard's nerve broke and he whirled to flee just as Fargo reached him. Fargo squeezed the trigger. But as fate would have it, at that exact split second, the man's rifle struck the derringer, throwing off Fargo's aim. The slug meant for the guard's head sizzled through empty space.

The man's eyes were wild with panic. He drove the stock at Fargo's face, shrieking, "Not me you won't! Not me!"

Fargo dodged but the stock still caught him on the shoulder. He was slow. His reflexes, his strength, were not what they should be. Understandable, given that his body had not had time to recover from the torture. He swung his right fist. Normally when he hit someone on the jaw, it jolted them. But all the guard did was blink, then try to bash his skull in.

Half a dozen captives were down but the rest were pressing Lester and the other guard. Their ghastly forms, their strange silence, gave the illusion they were not quite human.

"Let's get out of here!" the man next to Lester squawked, and ran straight into the ring of outstretched talons.

Fargo glimpsed all this as he sidestepped another blow. He kicked out with his right foot and caught the man's knee. The man cried out and stumbled. Swift as thought, Fargo hit him in the throat, once, twice, three times. That was enough.

The guard next to Lester was on the ground, cadavers clawing and tearing and pounding at him. Bony fingers around his throat were choking off his breath. He had lost his rifle and was struggling to rise, but as weak as they were, there were too many for him.

Lester had emptied his rifle and spun to flee. He had not seen Fargo pick up the rifle of the third guard. When he turned, he spun directly into its muzzle. He stopped, transformed to stone, and hissed, "No!"

"Yes," Fargo said, and blew off the top of his head.

Choking sounds issued from the final guard, who was covered with spectral avengers. His legs flailed wildly, went rigid, quivered violently, and were abruptly and permanently still.

The ground was littered with bodies. Fargo counted eight dead captives, three of them women. Calista, thankfully, was not one of them. Those still alive were standing and staring at the guards as if they could not quite believe the guards were indeed dead.

"We did it," Edgar Rice breathlessly declared. "After all this time, we honest to God did it."

"We're free of this place." Rob Howard grinned. "We can get on with our lives. It's over at last."

"Wrong," Fargo said loud enough for all to hear. "It's just beginning."

"How do you figure, mister?" a woman asked.

"Cole Narciss can't let word of what went on here get out. He will be after you to silence you."

"I just want to go home," a different woman said.

"I want my store back," Edgar Rice stated.

Several more started to talk at once, and Fargo quieted them with a gesture. "You must be patient. We can't end this in one night."

"Tell us what to do and we will do it," Calista assured him.

The others voiced agreement. As one animated skeleton put it, "There aren't many of us and we're weak as kittens, but we'll do our part. We couldn't live with ourselves if we didn't." Choked with emotion, he shook a bony fist. "The vermin who did this to us must pay!"

Fargo couldn't agree more.

15

There was a lot to do. They had to move fast. Fargo doubted the shots had been heard in Wet Grass, not when it was close to two in the morning. But Wet Grass was only a mile away, and some people were light sleepers.

He rattled off instructions. He had the children ushered out of the pen to the campfire. He had women gather up all the blankets they could carry. Others took the food from the cache under the lean-to, and the water skin. He passed out three of the rifles and kept one for himself. The same with the revolvers and the gun belts. He found his Arkansas toothpick on Lester and slid it into his ankle sheath.

A store-bought shirt off one of the dead guards was the only shirt that would fit him, and not too well. He helped himself to socks and a pair of boots, the socks a size too small, the boots too loose. A black hat had to do until he recovered his own clothes.

In the meantime, the captives were busy tearing down lean-tos and spreading the dry branches along the fence.

At a word from Fargo, the remaining lean-tos and the fence were set on fire. Many of the captives smiled and excitedly clapped their hands as the flames rapidly spread. Some wanted to stay and watch the pen burn to the ground, but Fargo pointed out the danger.

"The night riders might show up. We must be long gone or all we've done will be for nothing."

Four mounts belonging to the guards were picketed

nearby. Fargo claimed a roan for himself and gave the other three to the other men with rifles: Edgar Rice, Rob Howard, and one other man.

Fargo led the exodus. They traveled north across the benighted prairie in a long line, the women and children moving as briskly as their wasted conditions allowed. Edgar was off to the right, Rob Howard to the left. The fourth man brought up the rear.

A short discussion before they set out resulted in a mutual decision to head for Calista Baxter's farm. The house was large enough to hold all of them, the windows had shutters with firing slots, and her root cellar contained ample food. In short, they could hole up indefinitely. And, too, it was near enough to the Oregon Trail that a watcher in the barn hayloft could go for help should any wagons or riders happen by.

The captives were in good spirits, happier than any of them had been in months. But Fargo did not share in their elation. They had escaped the pen, but there were Cole Narciss and Pyle Kutyer to deal with, to say nothing of the night riders.

The slow pace wreaked havoc with Fargo's nerves. His natural impulse was to hurry the women and children along, but they were doing the best they could. Calista was carrying Susie, who had fallen asleep.

They had been on the move for half an hour when a big-boned woman tramped up next to Fargo's mount. "See here, mister. What's the meaning of this?"

"I can't read minds," Fargo said when she did not go on.

"Why are you men on horseback and us women must walk? Some of us can ride, you know, and we are in a lot worse shape than you are." She sniffed in disdain. "It is not very gentlemanly of you. Not very gentlemanly at all."

"Would it be gentlemanly to let the night riders kill you?"

"What? No. Of course not." The woman made it sound like the most ridiculous question she ever heard. "What do they have to do with it?"

"Everything," Fargo patiently explained. "From up

here I can see farther. I can spot trouble before it reaches us, and head it off faster."

"Oh. It's to protect us better?" The big-boned woman deflated. "My apologies." She drifted back to rejoin the others.

Shortly after, Rob Howard trotted over from his position on the flank. "I think I saw something."

"You think?" Fargo reminded himself the man was a saloon owner and not a scout.

"West of us. Riders maybe, heading south in a hurry. But they were too far off for me to be sure."

"You take the lead," Fargo directed. "Fire three shots in the air if you need me."

"Where will you be?"

Fargo did not answer. It should be obvious. He rode for a long while, but saw nothing other than stars and waving grass and heard nothing other than the wind. Eventually he came within sight of the fence, parts of which were still burning. He was about convinced it had been Rob Howard's imagination. Then silhouettes appeared against the glare of the distant flames. Riders, more than a few, roving about.

Searching for them, Fargo warranted. The captives had to be warned. But he did not rush to warn them; he rode toward the pen.

A torch flared. Then another. And yet a third. The torches were held close to the ground and moved back and forth. The men holding them were searching for tracks. The men were wearing burlap hoods.

Fargo had to discourage them. As soon as he was within rifle range, he reined up and dismounted. The rifle he had taken from the dead guard was a Sharps, a heavy-caliber model suitable for downing buffalo. He had used one himself before he switched to the Henry.

The torches were about where the gate had been. It would not take the searcher long to find the trail.

Fargo wedged the Sharps to his shoulder. The sights were next to useless at night. He had to rely on instinct. He aimed at the vague form of one of the men holding the torches, and thumbed back the hammer.

Thunder rolled across the plain. The torch dropped to the grass. Distant cries and shouts betokened anger and confusion.

Climbing back on, Fargo rode a hundred yards to the southeast. By then someone had picked up the fallen torch and the three torches were again sweeping back and forth.

Fargo did not climb down this time. In his pocket were cartridges he had taken from the dead guard. He reloaded, then took aim at a spot about two feet above a torch. The instant after he fired, he reined to the north. It was well he did. The men by the fence let loose a volley, firing at the Sharps's muzzle flash. Had Fargo not moved, he or the roan or both might have taken a slug.

Again Fargo drew rein. Faint curses reached him. He fed in a new cartridge and waited for the torches to move about. Instead, all three were extinguished.

Fargo figured the men at the pen would lie low a while, then continue their search. So he stayed where he was. Several minutes went by. He discovered he was mistaken when the roan abruptly raised its head and pricked its ears. He sensed what it was about to do before it did it, but had no chance to clamp his hand over its muzzle.

The roan whinnied.

Off in the dark a horse answered. As if that were a stage cue, shots smashed out, seven or eight rifles in crashing cadence.

Wrenching on the reins, Fargo jabbed his heels and was off like a rabbit spooked by a coyote. He galloped north, toward Wet Grass, not to the northeast, toward Calista's farm. He hoped to lead the night riders away from the captives.

The roan surprised him. It was not as fast as the Ovaro but it was not a turtle, either. The hooves that pounded in pursuit did not close the gap. He glanced back a few times but saw only indistinct movement. When he was a third of a mile from the settlement he swung to the west, and after racing a couple of hundred yards, he drew rein.

Cat and mouse.

Fargo held the roan's bridle and covered its muzzle

and hoped to heaven it would not give him away a second time. Soon horsemen pounded by, making for Wet Grass. His ruse had worked. He tried to count them but it was too dark. He did see a few clearly enough to distinguish their hoods. When the hammering faded, he forked leather and trotted east.

He had bought the captives extra time. They should be able to reach Calista's farm without incident. But since it was never wise to take anything for granted, he pushed the roan and came within sight of the two-story stone-and-log farmhouse shortly before dawn. The place appeared deserted. But as he neared the weed-choked yard and an overgrown flower garden, a face appeared at a downstairs window, and a second later the front door flew open and Calista rushed out to greet him.

"You're safe!"

The emotion in her voice surprised him. So did the hug she gave him when he climbed down.

"We were worried," she said softly. "If not for you, we would still be in that awful pen, dying a little each day."

"Don't make more of it than there was." Fargo led the roan toward the barn.

"If you ask me, we can never make enough."

Fargo opened one of the wide double doors. The other three horses were in stalls. He placed the roan in the first stall on the left but did not strip off the saddle.

Calista noticed. "Are you planning to head out again soon?"

"In an hour," Fargo revealed. Time enough for the roan to rest and to get some food into his stomach.

"Why? You just got here. What is so important it can't wait?"

"Our lives." Fargo loosened the cinch, closed the stall, and walked out into the golden advent of a new day. It occurred to him that he had been up all night. But he did not feel tired. To the contrary: he was bursting with vigor.

Calista would not look at him as they crossed to the house. She was troubled about something. She gave him no clue as to what it might be until they were climbing the steps to the porch. "After this is all over I hope you will stick around a day or two."

"I just might," Fargo said. The ladies at the saloon were friendly enough. Cat and Pinky were downright playful, and he had yet to find out exactly *how* playful.

"I have an extra bedroom," Calista went on quickly. "You are welcome to use it for as long as you like."

"What would your neighbors think?" Fargo joked.

"I honestly don't care. Once I would have." Calista nervously played with her hair. "That was before all this. Before I learned what is important in life and what isn't."

No one needed to beat Fargo over the head with a singletree for him to divine her motive. "Just don't expect more than I can give you."

"Oh, I won't. Honest," Calista replied. "A day or two is all I ask. To remind me."

Fargo had needed reminding himself a few times. "I can't make any promises, but I will if I can."

Calista beamed to rival the sun.

The tantalizing aromas of cooking food and brewing coffee practically had Fargo drooling as he entered the house. They were all there, temporarily safe and deliriously happy at their deliverance. Between the front door and the kitchen a dozen hands clapped him on the arm or the back. A chair was vacated at the kitchen table so he could sit. A woman Fargo had never talked to brought him a steaming cup of coffee and the sugar bowl.

Here in the farmhouse, where a typical family had once lived a normal life, the ghoulish state of the captives was all the more apparent and unsettling. That they had survived was a miracle, and they were making up for their deprivation. The pump out back could not work fast enough to slake their thirst. The pantry and the root cellar were the most popular haunts in the house. Everything from soup to bacon to bread was being cooked or baked.

Fargo was taking a sip of the near-scalding coffee when Edgar Rice and Rob Howard leaned on separate corners of the table.

"We've been talking it over and we have come to a decision," Edgar Rice announced.

Rob Howard nodded. "We have to stop Cole Narciss."

"I'm open to suggestions," Fargo told them.

"It's simple," Edgar Rice said. "We stay here a couple of days to get our strength back. Then we ride into Wet Grass and blast that conniving maggot to hell."

"The two of you?" Fargo said. "Narciss has a lot of hired guns working for him." About the same number, Fargo reflected, as the number of night riders. Some would call that coincidence. Not Fargo.

"Give us more credit," Edgar Rice was saying. "The other two men who made it out of the pen alive are with us. If we include you, that gives us five guns."

"Nowhere near enough," Fargo said. "And you're forgetting that as far as the good citizens of Wet Grass are concerned, all of you have been exposed to smallpox. They might shoot you themselves."

"It's a risk we're willing to take," Rob Howard declared.

"But not one I am," Fargo said.

"Why not?" Edgar Rice demanded. "We can pay Narciss a visit late at night when he is alone in his house. One shot to the brain or the heart and this vile madness is finally over."

"Except for the smallpox and the night riders," Fargo pointed out the flaw in their logic.

"Narciss is more important," Rob Howard said.

Fargo took a few more sips of coffee. "You're not fooling anyone," he quietly commented.

"Who says we're trying to?" Edgar Rice demanded.

"The real reason you two are so all-fired anxious to get yourselves killed is because you want your businesses back," Fargo said.

Edgar Rice glowered. "Can you blame us? Narciss took everything we own in this world."

"And we'll be damned if we'll let him get away with it," Rob Howard declared.

An argument loomed. Just then, little Susie rushed into the kitchen and over to Fargo. She clasped his hand.

"Come quick! Hurry!"

"What for?" Fargo was perfectly content there. "And

where is your mother?" The last he saw of Calista, she had headed up the stairs to the second floor.

"She sent me," Susie said. "She saw them out the window and told me to come fetch you."

"Saw who?" Fargo asked.

"The bad men who want to kill us."

16

The upstairs window faced west, toward Wet Grass.

Fargo thought the girl meant the night riders had found them, but there were only three riders and they were not wearing hoods. Pyle Kutyer was one. The other two were also familiar: Ben and Darnell, two of Fargo's sparring partners from the fight at the saloon, the ones who had delivered him to the pen in their guise as night riders. They were still a ways off and taking their sweet time.

"Why is Kutyer coming here?" Calista wondered aloud. "My husband and I never had any dealings with him."

Fargo had a more important concern. "Is everyone inside the house?"

"So far as I know."

"Pull all the window shades. Make sure all the windows and doors are locked and tell everyone to stay away from the windows. Maybe they will ride by and not notice we are here." Fargo tried to remember if the barn doors were open. He followed Calista downstairs and went into the parlor. A window there faced the barn. The barn doors were closed. He was turning when Edgar Rice and Rob Howard rushed into the room.

"What is this we hear about Pyle Kutyer and a couple of gun sharks?" Edgar Rice inquired.

"They will be here in a couple of minutes," Fargo confirmed.

"What are we waiting for?" Rob Howard asked.

"Grab your rifle. As soon as they ride into the yard, we'll cut them down."

"One might get away," Fargo said. "It's better they don't know we're here. Word might reach Narciss."

"I'm not scared of him," Edgar Rice declared.

"Me either," Rob Howard said.

"I wasn't thinking of you. I was thinking of the women and children." Fargo would do all he could to spare them further hell. "If Narciss finds out, he and his pack of wolves will surround the house."

"Then what do you suggest?" Edgar Rice demanded. "That we do nothing? That we let the chance pass?"

"All I ask is that you be patient a few days longer," Fargo said. "I hope to get some help from the settlement."

Rob Howard swore. "All right. For the sake of the women and the kids, we'll go along, for now. But I don't like it. I don't like it one bit."

Fargo had left the Sharps leaning against the kitchen table. While Calista and the others scurried about closing curtains and bolting windows and doors, he slipped out the back door and glided around the corner. Lilac bushes near the front were convenient cover. He crouched and removed the black hat.

Pyle, Ben, and Darnell were several hundred yards out, holding to a slow walk. They were talking and smiling and gave no indication they thought anyone was there.

Fargo took a bead on Pyle Kutyer. The others were small fry. If shooting did break out, Kutyer wasn't leaving alive.

The trio stared at the house. Fargo hoped to hell the others were staying away from the windows. He relaxed a little when none of the three showed any alarm. They came to within thirty feet and drew rein.

"So this is the one you want?" asked Ben, the hardcase with the crooked nose.

Pyle Kutyer nodded. His jacket was open, and the pearl-handled grips to his Remington gleamed in the bright morning sun.

"I'm surprised he's letting you have it," Darnell said. His hat was pulled low over his big ears. "He's keeping all the rest for himself."

"He's short on cash. He has enough to pay you boys, but my services cost more. A lot more. So he's letting me keep it or sell it, whichever I decide."

"You never struck me as a plow-pusher," Darnell said.

"I'd rather be shot," Kutyer admitted. "But it might be nice to have a place I can come back to between jobs. Somewhere I know is safe."

"I need more excitement than that settlement offers," Ben commented.

"If things go as the boss says they will," Darnell said, "it won't be a settlement forever."

Fargo's interest quickened. He mentally filed the comment for later consideration and strained to hear more.

"We should head over to the Oregon Trail and keep a lookout for that wagon train," Pyle Kutyer said. "It's due any day now."

"Why is he so interested in it?" Ben asked.

"Someone with important information is supposed to be on one of the wagons," Pyle Kutyer revealed.

"I wish we knew what it was all about," Darnell grumbled. "He keeps everything to himself."

"All I care about is being paid," Ben said.

They gigged their mounts to the south. Fargo stayed in the lilacs until they were out of sight, then donned the black hat and walked to the front door. Calista opened it for him.

Edgar Rice was peering out a window. "I hated to do that," he said. "Let them ride off when we had them in our gun sights."

"I'm leaving," Fargo announced. "I expect to be back by nightfall. If not, if you don't hear from me, a wagon train is coming up the trail soon. Watch for them. Ask their help."

"Where are you going?" asked Rob Howard.

Fargo pretended he had not heard. He was outside and halfway to the barn when footsteps pattered and Calista's hand found his arm.

"Must you go?"

"It can't be helped or I wouldn't." Pausing, Fargo glanced at the house, then lowered his voice. "Keep an eye on Rice and Howard. They might try something that will put the rest of you in danger."

"What?"

"There's no predicting," Fargo said. "But if they disappear, have everyone hide in the timber along the Platte River." He squeezed her hand and hurried into the barn. It was a long ride to Wet Grass.

The settlement lay deceptively tranquil under the burning sun. The street was practically empty. Fargo counted on that, and the fact that he was wearing different clothes and riding a different horse. As an added precaution, he had circled and entered Wet Grass from the west. He was almost to the saloon when he reined into a space between two buildings and rode past the back of the saloon and on to the rear of the house where Jasmine had her apartment.

His hand on the Smith and Wesson he had taken from a dead guard, Fargo went up the stairs and along the hall to Jasmine's room. It was early yet, and she should still be there. He knocked, lightly. There was no response so he knocked again.

"Who is it?"

"Yell a little louder, why don't you?" Fargo said, hoping no one had heard her. The door flew open and Jasmine yanked him into the room. Her arms enfolded his neck and her soft lips molded to his. He shut the door behind him.

After a while Jasmine stepped back. She was in her chemise and cotton drawers. "God, you look awful," she said huskily. "And those clothes you're wearing stink to high heaven. What happened? Where did the night riders take you?"

"First things first." Fargo saw his shirt, hat, socks, and boots in a neat pile in the corner, next to his Henry. He began stripping off the clothes he had taken from the guards.

"Is my horse still in the stable?"

"I wouldn't know," Jasmine said. She put a hand on his naked chest. "I've been so worried. I went to the saloon and tried to get people to help look for you. The only ones who would were those two adorable puppies, Billy Flate and Matt Dancer, and some of the farmers. Steve Sherwood, John Busby, Glenn Handy, and Russ Cepna. They searched around for the better part of a day."

"Where are they now?"

"Flate and Dancer might be in the saloon. They're low on money, and Jim and Jackie Fina have been staking them to eats. Pinky Belle has been fussing over them, too, but she's a regular mother hen." Jasmine paused. "The rest might be out at the Sherwood farm. They've banded together to protect themselves from the night riders, and all their wives are at his place."

Fargo remembered Sherwood saying he had something important to tell him.

"If they are not there, I don't know where they would be."

Fargo had removed everything except his buckskin pants. He turned to the pile but Jasmine slipped in front of him. A mischievous smile curled those luscious lips of hers.

"What's your hurry, handsome?"

"I can't stay." Fargo had more to do before he returned to Calista's.

Jasmine leaned close, her breath warm on his skin, and traced the edge of his right ear with her finger. "You can't spare a few hours?"

"Not even half an hour," Fargo said.

"How about ten minutes?" Jasmine asked, and brazenly placed her other hand on the part of him that often had a mind of its own.

Despite himself, Fargo stirred. "You are a shameless hussy."

"And damn proud of it." Jasmine voice had grown sultry with desire. She massaged him, down low, and said softly, "How about it? Ten minutes isn't asking much."

Fargo supposed he could spare the time. He kissed her, lightly. His lower lip was still split and sore. His whole body, for that matter, had more aches and pains than he cared to count. The saloon brawl and the fight at the pen had left plenty of bruises. But he forgot about them as Jasmine pressed her hourglass form against his rock-hard muscles. She was soft and yielding in all the right places. Her perfume was a bed of roses and a field of daisies rolled into one.

Soon Fargo's muscles were not the only thing that was hard.

For her part, Jasmine kissed and licked and stroked him in wanton hunger. She was not in the least shy or inhibited. She was one of those women to whom making love was an ordinary part of life. An outlook Fargo respected. He was not one of those who regarded sharing a bed with a woman as evil or sinful.

Jasmine's velvet tongue enclosed an earlobe. Her fingers entwined in his hair while her other hand roved.

Fargo guided her toward the bed. She had said ten minutes and he was going to hold her to it. She eagerly slid onto her back and grinned as he eased onto his knees.

"I haven't stopped thinking about the other night," Jasmine said softly. "You could get to be a habit with a girl."

Undoing her drawers, Fargo slid them off and dropped them to the floor. Her chemise joined it.

Naked, Jasmine was exquisite. Cascading red hair, emerald eyes, the cherry hue of her lips, the ivory sheen of her throat, and the swell of her ample breasts were enough to bring a lump to any man's throat. To say nothing of her rust-hued thatch and the creamy sheen of her thighs. She was everything a man could desire, and she was his for the taking.

Bending, Fargo covered a breast with his mouth and lightly nipped the nipple. She moaned and arched her back, her fingernails digging into his shoulders. Placing his right palm on her leg, he massaged her pliant thigh from her knee to within a few inches of her slit.

Jasmine moved her bottom in a seductive invitation and husked, "I want you so much. You have no idea."

Fargo switched to her other breast. Both heaved with yearning. Her ankles slid behind him and rubbed the backs of his legs. When he covered her core with his hand, she threw her head back, her mouth a red oval, but did not utter a sound. That changed when he lightly ran a fingertip along her moist nether lips. Her groan filled the room.

"There! Touch me there!"

Fargo went her one better. He slid his finger into her honeypot. Jasmine quivered, and would not stop. He plunged his finger in and out, eliciting moans and throaty purrs. They grew louder the faster he plunged. Jasmine fastened her mouth to his so hard it hurt. By then he was feeling more pleasure than pain, and didn't care.

Parting her legs, Jasmine reached for him. Her fingers were warm, experienced, arousing. In no time she had him on the verge of exploding. His expression provoked a grin. "Why, Skye Fargo. You look as if you could eat me alive."

Fargo grinned.

"Do you want me to do the honors or will you?" Jasmine teased. "Not that I mind, but my ma raised me to have manners."

Fargo laughed, and rammed up into her. She had not realized he was poised for the thrust and it caught her off guard. Her eyes wide in rapture, she about came off the bed. Gripping her hips, Fargo pumped his own. The sensations that shot through him were the sensations men lived for.

"Yes. Oh, yes," Jasmine breathed. "I want it faster. I want it harder. As hard as you can."

Fargo nearly split her in twain. But she loved it. She clung to his shoulders and lavished molten kisses on his mouth and chin and neck, her body moving in perfect accord with his own. Gradually the ebb and flow of their mutual lust rose to a fever pitch. The bed creaked madly under them. Fargo's bruises protested the rough treatment but their protests were drowned in his rising tide of ecstasy.

Fargo once heard a madam at a bawdy house say that sex was ambrosia for the body. She was right. It was that, and it was more. It lofted a man to the heights of living and was as potent, in its way, as the best whiskey.

Jasmine cried out when she gushed. It was the trigger for Fargo's own release. Together they crested. Together they floated back to earth and lay side by side, panting.

"My oh my," Jasmine mewed. "If I could chain you to my bedpost and keep you forever, I would." Her gaze strayed past him, and she was seized by sudden and unexpected fright.

With a start, Fargo realized that when he closed the door he had forgotten to throw the bolt. He rolled onto his back, knowing what he would see before he saw it.

Someone was slowly, stealthily opening the door.

17

Fargo's hand stabbed for the Smith and Wesson. He had it level and was applying pressure to his thumb to curl back the hammer when the doorway was filled by a blond bundle of femininity in a dress so tight it was a wonder she could breathe.

"Oh, my!" Cat Sultraine declared. "Don't tell me I have interrupted you two playing doctor and nurse." Her eyes lingered on Fargo. "Mercy. Is that a redwood I see?"

By then Jasmine had found her voice. "Don't you ever knock?"

"You said to meet you here and we would go to the saloon together," Cat responded. "How was I to know you were entertaining?"

"You could at least shut the door. My landlord would have a fit if he saw me like this."

Grinning, Cat shut the door and leaned against it. "So how many times did you gush? The most I ever have is four. But he was special."

Jasmine sat up and leaned over the bed to snatch her chemise and drawers. "You would think this was a bordello, the way you carry on."

"Don't mind me, you two," Cat bantered. "Pretend I'm not here and carry on."

Fargo stood and hitched at his pants. "I have to go." He stepped to the corner and hurriedly began dressing.

"Don't rush off on my account."

A sound reminiscent of a strangled goose came from Jasmine. "Throw yourself at him, why don't you?"

"I didn't hear you screaming rape," Cat countered.

A rap on the door intruded on the tiff. Cat Sultraine peeked out, chuckled, and admitted a living testament to the color pink. "Pinky! You just missed it. Jasmine was giving this tall drink of water lessons in how to pass the time with a woman of ill repute."

"And I missed it, you say?" Pinky pretended to be crestfallen. "Maybe it's just as well. The sight of a naked man might turn my hair white."

Cat and Pinky laughed.

Fargo had his shirt and hat on. His boots took some tugging. Except for the missing Colt, he was back to his old self. He hefted the Henry and nodded at Jasmine. "I'll treat you to a drink when this is over."

"What about me? I like brandy as much as the next gal," Cat said, playfully batting her long eyelashes.

"I'm more partial to mint juleps," Pinky said. "And I'd sure like to find out if you are as hairy below the neck as you are above it."

"Her and her hair," Jasmine muttered.

"So long as it's not nose hairs," Pinky amended.

Fargo was glad to escape. He went down the stairs at the back. Taking the roan's reins, he headed for the stable. He did not skulk behind the buildings. He went between them to the main street and walked down the middle of the street so everyone would see him, the Henry in the crook of his elbow.

To Fargo's great relief, the Ovaro was there. Leaning the Henry against the stall, he threw on the saddle blanket and reached for his saddle.

From out of the room at the back came the stableman. He had a sheaf of papers and a pencil. "There you are. I was beginning to wonder what had happened to you." When Fargo did not respond, he said, "Remember me? Jeff Crom? I was here when you brought your pinto in."

"I remember." Fargo stood so he could keep an eye on the double doors. Word was bound to spread that he was back.

"I sure do like that horse of yours. I sketched him. See?" Crom held out a remarkable likeness of the Ovaro. "You can keep it if you want." When Fargo went on saddling the pinto, he said, "One day I hope to go back east and make my living as an artist."

From down the street came hollering. Fargo could not quite make out what was being yelled.

"You're not a gabby cuss, are you?" Crom asked.

"I have my moments," Fargo said. "I'm obliged for the sketch." He folded it and slid it into a saddlebag.

"There's something else," Crom said, with a sharp glance out the wide double doors. "Two men were in here about twenty minutes ago asking about your animal."

"Oh?"

"They wanted to know when you would be back to claim it. I told them I had no idea and they got mad."

"You wouldn't happen to know their handles?"

"One goes by Ben and the other calls himself Darnell. They work for Cole Narciss. Pushy types, especially that Ben. I had half a mind to shove a pitchfork up his ass."

Shadows flitted across the entrance.

The last Fargo knew, Darnell and Ben were supposed to be with Kutyer somewhere along the Oregon Trail, waiting for a wagon train. Why had they returned to Wet Grass so soon? "Where is your pitchfork?" he asked.

Jeff Crom gave him a strange look and pointed. It was leaning against the front wall to the right of the doors.

Fargo hugged the shadows. The pitchfork handle was sturdy, and the tines were coated with horse manure.

Not five seconds elapsed, and the shadows outside strode into the stable. Ben and Darnell had their revolvers out and bloodlust in their eyes. Only in Ben's case, it was Fargo's Colt, which they had taken from him the night they jumped him at Jasmine's apartment. They stopped when they saw the stableman.

"Where the hell is Skye Fargo?" Ben demanded. "We saw him come in here so don't try to lie to us."

"I'm right here," Fargo said, and when the pair whirled, he buried the tines in Ben's chest. Almost in the same motion, Fargo grabbed Ben's wrist and twisted, and the Colt fell from fingers gone limp. Faster than thought, the Colt was in Fargo's hand.

Astonishment slowed Darnell. "You!" he bleated.

"Me," Fargo said, and shot him in the gut.

Darnell staggered, clutched himself, and doubled over. The color draining from his face, he screeched, "Damn you to hell!"

"You first." Fargo shot him in the head.

Jeff Crom looked like he had sat on a porcupine. "You killed them!"

"That was the general idea."

"Two hardcases, just like that." Crom snapped his fingers, and chortled. "If I was as good as you, I might give up art and wear a tin star."

"Do you own a revolver?" Fargo asked.

"Sure don't," the stableman said. "On what I get paid, I can barely afford my art supplies."

Fargo drew the Smith and Wesson, and gripped it by the barrel. "You own one now."

"For me?" Crom said in delight. He held the revolver in one hand and the pencil and papers in the other. "Which to choose?"

Silence had fallen over Wet Grass. Fargo's spurs jangled as he walked to the Ovaro, reloading as he went. He adjusted the cinch, tied his bedroll on, and shoved the Henry into the saddle scabbard.

"What do I do with the bodies?" Crom asked.

"Chop them up and feed them to any hungry hogs you can find." The saddle creaked as Fargo stepped into the stirrups.

"You're joshing, right?"

"Wrap them in blankets and leave them on Cole Narciss's front porch. If he asks what you are doing, tell him they are a gift from me."

"Are you sure you want me to do that? He'll be awful mad."

"He's going to be madder." Fargo flicked the reins and rode out of the stable. He did not rein east toward Calista's. He rode down the center of the street to the saloon hitch rail. Climbing down, he looped the reins around the rail. He had expected the saloon to be fairly empty, as early as it was. But it was doing brisk business. Men lined the bar, men filled the tables.

The murmur of conversation stopped when Fargo entered. All eyes swung toward him. Some of the expressions were guarded, wary. Some were friendly. A few were filled with disbelief and hate.

Fargo shouldered to the bar. The men on either side suddenly became eager to be somewhere else. Since he was putting on a show, Fargo thumped the bar and loudly demanded, "Whiskey."

Jim Fina brought a bottle, saying, "It's good to see you again. Rumor had it the night riders got hold of you."

"The rumor was right," Fargo said. He had barely begun to pour when a commotion behind him suggested a space was being cleared. He went on pouring. When the glass was full, he casually raised it to his lips and savored a swallow. Then he turned, his elbows on the bar.

The pair were cast in the same flinty mold as all of their kind. Fargo did not recognize them. That they had decided to brace him suggested they had burlap hoods stashed somewhere.

"Something I can do for you?"

"You're supposed to be under quarantine," the husky one on the right said.

The other nodded. "You were in the pen but you escaped. We're taking you with us."

Fargo wondered where that would be, with the pen burned to cinders. "Did you know?" he asked.

"Know what?" the husky tough responded.

"That when you woke up today, it would be the last day of your life?"

They looked at one another and grinned. They lived by the gun so they thought they were good with the gun. They thought they could beat him. Their hands swooped like diving hawks.

Fargo had the Colt out before they cleared leather. He shot the one on the right, shifted, and shot the one on the left. Both were head shots. He did not try to wing them. He did not cover them and demand they drop their hardware. He shot the bastards dead, and after their bodies stopped twitching, he calmly reloaded, twirled the Colt into his holster, and picked up his drink.

The patrons were numb with amazement. They were not strangers to death, what with all that had happened of late. But the suddenness of it left them mentally breathless.

"Now then," Fargo began to get their attention. "I have a story to tell. You will sit and listen." And as pools of blood formed under the freshly deceased gun sharks, and a clock *tick-tick-ticked* on the far wall, Fargo told them about the quarantine pen, about its conditions, about the people who had been held there. He spared no detail of the suffering, the ravaged bodies.

A horrified silence gripped the listeners. No one spoke. No one coughed. No one took so much as a sip of liquor.

When he was done, Fargo set the glass on the bar. "This is your settlement, not mine. You live here. You farm the land. You have the most to lose if nothing is done." He paused. "Those are your friends at the Baxter farm. They need your help. They need it now." He stepped to the dead men. "Do you see these two? They were night riders. Their friends are going to try and kill your friends. Who will ride with me to stop them?"

A settler at a table cleared his throat. "What's it all about, mister? I can't make hide nor hair of what is going on and who is behind it."

"I'm not sure of all the details, myself," Fargo admitted, then stressed, "The important thing are those poor people out at Calista's."

From the back of the saloon came the two young men, Billy Flate and Matt Dancer. Neither lived there. Neither had a stake in it. Yet Billy Flate grinned and said, "Hell, mister. You can count me and my pard in. We like excitement almost as much as we like making cow eyes at pretty fillies."

Matt Dancer bobbed his chin. "That's right. Besides, we've been down under that Cole Narciss's thumb for weeks now, what with him not letting us leave. It's got me as hopping mad as a koala."

"Don't you mean a kangaroo?" Billy Flate said.

"I get them confused," Dancer replied.

Farmers came forward next, a knot of them, most men Fargo had already met: John Busby, Steve Sherwood, Glenn Handy, Russ Cepna, and others. Several from the settlement introduced themselves as Mark Hallam, Jason Zano, Randy Ore, and Jan Way. Before long Fargo was ringed by every man in the place.

"We'll do whatever you want, mister," Randy Ore said. "We're sick and tired of the killing, sick and tired of living in fear."

"What do you have in mind?" Mark Hallam asked.

Fargo told them. He had worked it out in his head on the ride in. His plan met with their approval. Soon those who lived in the settlement were hastening out to spread the news and get their guns.

Fargo went over to four farmers standing in their own little group; Handy, Cepna, Busby, and Sherwood. To the latter he said, "You mentioned the other night that you had something to tell me."

"It was about a month ago," Steve Sherwood said. "I was plowing a field and stayed out late. Well after sunset. There was a full moon and I had enough light to keep on plowing."

Fargo was not the only one listening. So was every other person in the saloon.

"I stopped about ten o'clock or so," Sherwood related. "I unhitched the plow horse and was heading home when I heard riders coming. I didn't have my rifle with me so I ducked into a stand of oaks. Pretty soon I saw them, plain as day. Them and their damn hoods. It was the night riders."

"Did they spot you?" John Busby asked.

"No. I was lucky. I got under cover in time. I was worried my horse would nicker and give me away, but it didn't."

When Sherwood did not go on, Fargo goaded him with, "Is that all there was to it?"

"Oh, no. You see, all the night riders were wearing hoods, except one. The man in the lead. Maybe he figured no one would be out and about that late. Maybe he figured no one would see him. But I was, and I did."

"Do you reckon it was their leader?" Glenn Handy asked.

"Judge for yourselves," Sherwood answered.

Fargo could have heard a pin drop.

"The man I saw that night, the man out in front of the night riders, the man without a hood, was Cole Narciss."

18

The sun was setting. Calista Baxter came running from her farmhouse as Fargo and his party approached. The anxiety on her face warned Fargo that something was wrong.

"I kept an eye on Rob and Edgar like you wanted me to," Calista said anxiously as Fargo reined up. "They didn't like standing around doing nothing. Then the lookout in the hayloft came to the house to report that he had seen someone in a hood spying on us from the woods to the north."

Fargo could guess what came next.

"Rob and Edgar got excited. They figured it must be a night rider, and if they could capture him, they could make him tell them who was behind it all. So they took the men with them and went off."

"*All* the men who were here?" Fargo swore.

Calista nodded. "I tried to talk them out of it. So did some of the other ladies. But they wouldn't listen. They said they could end this once and for all."

"How long ago was this?"

"Not more than an hour."

Fargo shifted in the saddle. "I'm going after them," he informed the group he had brought from Wet Grass. It consisted of Glenn Handy, Russ Cepna, Steve Sherwood, John Busby, Randy Ore, and the two young gold seekers, Flate and Dancer. "Hide your horses in the barn. Stay out of sight in the house, and be ready for anything."

133

"Do you think the night riders will show up while you are gone?" Glenn Handy asked.

"I hope not. But they were bound to figure out this is where the people from the pen came," Fargo said. "That's probably why they had someone watching the place."

"Let them come!" Matt Dancer declared. "I can lick my weight in tigers!"

"Shouldn't that be wildcats?" Billy Flate asked.

"Make it mammoths," Matt Dancer replied. "They weigh more."

Russ Cepna cleared his throat. "Are these two sane?"

"Is anyone?" John Busby said.

Calista looked up at Fargo. "Are they always like this? Or have they been drinking?"

"We haven't been eating oatmeal," Steve Sherwood told her.

Fargo sighed and flicked the reins. Time was crucial. It would be dark soon. He found where Howard and Rice and the other men had ridden due east from the barn, no doubt to mislead the watcher in the woods. Once they were in thick timber, they had circled to the north. The tracks showed where they had left their horses and crept on foot to take the watcher by surprise. But they were the ones who were surprised.

There had been more than one night rider. Over half a dozen had jumped the unsuspecting avengers. Torn ground and blood testified to the savagery of the fight. The upshot was that Howard and Rice and those with them, some badly wounded, were taken prisoner.

Sticking to the thickest vegetation, the night riders had gone west for half a mile, then headed due north. They were making for the Platte River, and for the wild tangle that bordered the winding river.

Twilight gave way to the black of night. Fargo could no longer track them unless he lit a torch, and a torch would give him away. He was debating whether to risk lighting one anyway when a shimmering orange finger off through the trees saved him the trouble. He had found the night riders.

Fargo left the Ovaro and advanced on foot. The last

hundred yards he traveled on his belly. He smelled the river.

The campfire was on a broad, grassy bank. Two night riders were seated beside it, drinking coffee and talking. Over near the edge of the bank lay six bound figures. None were moving or otherwise gave any sign of being alive.

Fargo crawled as near as he could. It was close enough to hear what was being said. The first thing he heard was a complaint.

"I hate these damn hoods."

"Quit your bellyaching," the second night rider said. "We're being paid top dollar, aren't we? And it's only burlap."

"Only," the first man said testily. "When I have it on, I sweat like a pig. And I can't hear like I normally do. If you ask me, we would better off wearing ladies' bonnets."

"Well, it won't be for much longer," the other said. "The boss thinks he can wrap this thing up in a day or two."

"He's been saying that for a while now," the second rider said. "So far all that's happened is he's taken over some farms and some property in Wet Grass. Not exactly what I would say is worth all this trouble."

"You think too small. You need to think bigger."

The second man growled in frustration. "I could wrestle with my noggin from now until the end of time and still not figure out what the boss is up to."

"What does it matter so long as we get paid?"

"That's all you care about, isn't it? The money. Me, I like to know what I'm risking my hide over."

"Bitch, bitch, bitch."

"I'm serious, damn it. Maybe you don't mind being kept in the dark but I do." The angry night rider gestured at the forms along the edge of the bank. "I don't want to end up like them and die without knowing why."

The other night rider was getting angry. "The next time the big man pairs me off with someone, it won't be you."

"What does that crack mean?"

There was more, but Fargo didn't listen. He circled to the right and rose in a crouch. They were so busy griping they did not hear him. Their first inkling came when he cocked the Colt.

Both night riders spun. Both held their hands over their six-shooters but did not draw.

"Not so much as a twitch," Fargo warned. "Do exactly as I tell you and only what I tell you and you go on breathing a while."

"How did you find us?" snapped the chronic complainer.

"When I said not so much as a twitch, that includes your mouth." Fargo came around behind them and relieved them of their revolvers, which he tossed over the bank into the Platte. "Where are the rest?"

The complainer tried to play dumb. "The rest of what?"

Fargo slugged him with the Colt. The man folded without a sound, a welt forming on his temple. Pointing the Colt at the other man, Fargo repeated his question.

"They're gone," the man said, sounding scared.

"Gone where?"

The man hesitated. "The boss didn't say."

Fargo backed toward the still forms at the edge of the bank. "What is Narciss up to? What is behind all this?"

"He's never told us. He says it's a secret."

Sinking to a knee, Fargo rolled over the first prisoner he came to. It was one of the men from the pen. He was dead. Shot between the eyes. Fargo rolled the next man over. Another survivor, likewise shot between the eyes. The same with the third. Fargo looked up. "Sons of bitches."

"It wasn't me!"

The next prone form was that of Edgar Rice. Fargo did not have to roll him over. A walnut-sized hole in the back of Rice's head left no doubt as to whether he was alive or dead.

"It was the big man!" the night rider exclaimed, in fear for his own life. "He had us lay them out in a row.

Then he went from one to the next, blowing their brains out."

"What's your name?"

"What?"

"You heard me," Fargo said.

"Syd. Sydney Oats. But everyone calls me Syd. My partner is Percy Nilo."

"Did either of you try to stop him?" Fargo asked.

"Stop who?"

"Who do you think?" Fargo rejoined, and shot Sydney Oats through the chest. He must have cored the heart because the man fell and never moved. Fargo bent over the fifth form on the rim. It was, as he expected, Rob Howard, minus a goodly portion of skull.

Fargo turned to the sixth and last form. He was momentarily puzzled. Only five men had survived the pen. Only five men besides himself had been at Calista's farm. Who was the sixth? he wondered. He rolled the man over and his puzzlement gave way to consternation. "It can't be!"

But it was. Cole Narciss, tied wrist and ankles, blood smeared in a dark stain on the left side of his head. As Fargo looked on in astonishment, Narciss stirred and blinked.

"What? Where?" The lord of Wet Grass glanced about him, settled on Fargo. "You! Where is he? Where is that no-good backstabbing son of a bitch?"

"Who?"

"Who else? Pyle Kutyer! He shot me and left me for dead. If I hadn't twisted my head, I'd be maggot food now." Narciss indulged in a string of words never heard in church. "I'm surprised he didn't finish me off."

"Maybe he thought he had," Fargo said, alluding to the blood.

"Cut me loose," Narciss said. "I have a score to settle."

Fargo sat back and coldly regarded the monster responsible for the bloodshed and suffering.

"Didn't you hear me? Cut me loose, damn it, so I can go after him! Or don't you care what Kutyer does?"

"I'll deal with him soon enough," Fargo said. "Right

now I want answers. Lots of answers. If I don't get them you can lie there and rot. Or until the wolves and coyotes get hungry."

Glowering, Narciss clenched his hands as if he were strangling someone. "Ask your damn questions."

Fargo posed the one uppermost on his mind, the one he had pondered since the beginning. "Why?"

"If I tell you, do you promise to let me go free?"

As the saying went, it would be a cold day in hell before that happened, but Fargo said, "I'll think about it."

Cole Narciss gnawed on his bottom lip. "I reckon I can't expect more than that. So the first answer you want is land. The land in the settlement and the farmland for ten miles around."

"You want it *all* for yourself?"

"Every square inch," Narciss confirmed. "Mine and no one else's."

"So you can rake in money at the saloon and general store from every wagon train that passes by?" To Fargo the reward did not justify the effort. Narciss would live comfortably enough, but it would never make him rich.

"I would never risk so much for so little." Narciss's features sharpened. "I'm after more than that. Much more."

"I'm listening." Fargo was anxious to uncover the mystery that clung to Wet Grass like a funeral shroud.

"You are a scout, I hear," Narciss said. "You've been to Fort Kearney and other posts along the frontier?"

"I've been to nearly every fort there is." Fargo was stating a simple fact, not bragging.

"Then you are familiar with the pattern," Narciss said. "A military post springs up, and the next thing a town is built around it and there are homesteads for miles around."

Fargo had witnessed the pattern many a time, and said so. "But that doesn't tell me why you want all the land in and around Wet Grass. There's no fort here."

"There will be," Narciss said. "The army needs another post. They can't properly protect the pilgrims bound for Oregon with the forts they have. They considered over a dozen sites and finally picked a spot near where Wet Grass is standing. But you know how slow the army works. The formal announcement won't be for another six months or more."

"How do you know all this?"

"I have a contact in the army. A cousin. He got word to me." Cole Narciss sat up. "Think of it. Settlers will flock here to be close to the fort. But I'll own all the land, and I won't sell cheap. I stand to make a fortune. Hundreds of thousands of dollars. But to get the land, I needed to drive off those who were already here. Drive them off or kill them. That's when I came up with the brainstorm of the smallpox."

Fargo was genuinely startled. "There is no epidemic?"

"Hell, no."

"I saw the Sunman family. They had the red splotches. I saw a man named Byerly. He had the splotches, too."

A laugh that gloried in the deviousness of its maker rippled from Cole Narciss. "You only thought they did. Red ink works wonders."

"But Byerly had other signs," Fargo noted. "He was so sick he could barely stand up."

"Larkspur," Narciss said.

Fargo was so shocked he lowered the Colt. "You poisoned them?" A common wild plant with beautiful flowers, every part of the gorgeous larkspur was poisonous. The toxin affected the heart and the nervous system. It worked quickly. Symptoms usually appeared within half an hour. If administered in large enough dosages, death came within hours. An extremely painful, horrible death.

"Them, and a lot of others," Narciss crowed. "It was easy as pie. My men would wait until a family left, then sneak into their house and mix larkspur with the food in their cupboard or pantry. Once the poison took effect, my men dabbed the red ink on the bodies, and skedaddled." He paused. "But it wasn't doing the job fast enough."

"So you came up with the idea of the night riders and the quarantine pen."

"Pretty clever, huh? And now you know almost all there is to know," Cole Narciss said.

"Almost? What else is there?"

Narciss grinned in vicious glee. "First, Percy is standing behind you with a six-gun aimed at your head. Second, you waltzed right into my trap." And with that, Cole Narciss cast off the rope that had seemingly bound his wrists, kicked, and stood up.

19

It was rare for Skye Fargo to be taken completely by surprise. He never imagined Cole Narciss was pretending to be tied up, never suspected the whole thing was a ruse to catch him off his guard. But it was, and it had worked, and now all he could do was stand there helpless as Narciss took the Colt from his hand and stepped back.

"I bet you're feeling godawful stupid right about now," the mastermind smirked. "You stepped right into my snare."

"You were lying there waiting for me," Fargo stated the obvious.

"Since sundown, yes," Narciss confirmed. "I knew you would come after me. I know your reputation as a tracker. It was only a question of time before you showed up."

Fargo's shock began to fade. He realized he must stall. "You went to a lot of trouble," he remarked.

"Mister, you don't know the half of it," Cole Narciss said. "You have been a thorn in my side since you arrived. At first I thought you were passing through. But when my men caught you spying near my house, I guessed the truth."

"What truth?"

"That someone sent you to find out what was going on. The army, I suspect. So I took steps to prevent you from getting word back to them. I had you placed in quarantine."

"But I *was* only passing through," Fargo said.

Cole Narciss raised the Colt to pistol-whip him but lowered it again. "Don't insult my intelligence. You have been working against me from the beginning. It can't have been by accident."

Fargo let him believe what he wanted. Shifting slightly, he saw that the night rider behind him was about six feet away. "Pyle Kutyer isn't trying to take over from you, is he?"

"If he did, he would be dead so fast, his head would swim," Cole Narciss bragged. "I said that to trick you."

Percy nervously cleared his throat. "Do I shoot this dandelion for you, boss?"

"In a minute, you clod. I will tell you when," Narciss replied. "I want to savor this moment."

Fargo tensed his legs.

"Yes, indeed," Cole Narciss crowed. "This turned out better than I dared hope. "With you dead, and the people from the pen wiped out—"

"What?" Fargo interrupted.

"Didn't I tell you? Pyle and the rest of my night riders are on their way to the Baxter farm even as we speak. I had suspected that was where the simpletons fled to. So I sent Pyle and a couple of other men to ride past the place earlier today. They saw someone peeking out a curtain."

"I've got to hand it to you," Fargo said. "You don't miss much."

"With so much money at stake, I should say not," Narciss declared. His smile was arctic ice and bobcat savagery rolled into one. "With you and those at the Baxter farm out of the way, I can carry out our plan."

"Not quite," Fargo said.

"Eh?"

"I went to Wet Grass. I told the settlers about the pen, about how people who did not have smallpox were kept there against their will, about Gront and Vole and all the rest."

Cole Narciss flushed with fury. "You did *what*?" He was so stunned that he lowered the Colt and reached out as if to grab the front of Fargo's shirt.

Fargo had hold of Narciss's wrist before Narciss could

blink. He whirled, swinging Narciss by the arm so that Narciss came between him and Percy. He thought that would keep the night rider from shooting long enough for him to leap and knock the man down. But Percy fired. The slug caught Cole Narciss low in the face, transforming his mouth into a red smear of mangled teeth and a severed tongue. Then Fargo had the Colt in his hand and was moving to the right for a clear shot at Percy.

Only Percy wasn't there.

The man had spun and bolted into the woods, bleating at the top of his lungs, "Oh my! Oh my! Oh my!"

Fargo did not go after him. He had little time to spare. Pyle Kutyer might already be at Calista's.

Gurgling rose at Fargo's feet. Cole Narciss was still alive and trying to speak. But all that came out of his blood-filled mouth was more blood. His eyes were wells of hate.

"All your scheming, all those you murdered," Fargo said. "What did it get you?"

Narciss's arm rose, his fingers hooked like claws. He groped wildly at Fargo's leg.

"You deserve a slow death. You deserve to die in the same agony as all those you poisoned, and those at the pen." Fargo aimed the Colt. "This is for them." He shot Narciss in the right knee, and Narciss blubbered and thrashed. When the thrashing slowed, Fargo shot him in the left knee. "That's so you don't go anywhere."

Narciss sputtered and gasped and rolled back and forth.

Fargo stepped to the fire. He carefully gripped the unlit end of a burning brand. Narciss had subsided and was lying weak and spent. Fargo held the brand so Narciss could see it. "I never like to kill. I only do it when I have to. But in your case, I will like it a lot."

Cole Narciss whined.

"Feel free to scream," Fargo said, and touched the brand to Narciss's expensive suit. Smoke blossomed. Tiny flames soon became large flames, and spread.

The first shriek was horrendous.

Fargo cast the brand into the fire and hurried to the Ovaro. More screams rent the night. He did not look back. Not until he was in the saddle and reining the pinto to the east.

There were two campfires, or so it seemed. One was writhing and twisting and weakly swatting itself.

The screams went on a good long while.

Fargo stopped listening. He had something else on his mind, namely, the fates of Calista and little Susie and the other women and children at the farm. He had left plenty of men to protect them, but the night riders outnumbered the protectors.

Above him, the stars crawled on their celestial path. The slowness with which they moved added to Fargo's unease.

He heard the shots long before he came within sight of the farm. Repeated flurries of blasts, rifles, and sidearms thundering in riotous cacophony. In a way it was encouraging. The people in the farmhouse were still alive. Some of them, at any rate.

A quarter of a miles west of the farmhouse, Fargo drew rein. The shooting had stopped. He slid the Henry from the saddle scabbard and a box of cartridges from his saddlebags. The box he crammed into a pocket. Then, levering a round into the rifle's chamber, he stalked forward.

The farmhouse was as dark and silent as a tomb. The barn doors were open but the interior was the color of ink.

Fargo smothered an urge to rush on in. Close to twenty rifles would cut him down before he got there. He scanned the tree line and the vicinity of the barn and the shrubs near the house, but he did not spot Kutyer or any of the night riders.

Exercising as much caution as a mountain lion stalking prey, Fargo worked his way along the edge of the trees. He figured if he could reach the barn undetected, a short dash would take him to the house.

Low to the ground, using available cover, Fargo circled halfway to the barn. Movement ahead brought him to a stop. He flattened and braced for an outcry but there was none. Muffled voices reached him. The voices of men speaking through burlap hoods. With painstaking caution, he crawled until he could hear them clearly.

"—rush in and get it over with."

"There's enough starlight for them to pick us off, is why we don't. Pyle has the right idea. Its best to wait until daybreak."

"What I don't get," said a third voice, "is who else is in there? I heard men yelling. But the boss caught Howard and Rice and those others. There aren't supposed to be any men here."

"It's a puzzlement," the second night rider agreed.

"Whoever it is will wish they hadn't butted in," said the first man. "It should be fun when Pyle springs his surprise."

The three laughed.

Skirting them, Fargo soon discovered that night riders were positioned every twenty yards or so along the tree line. They had the house and barn surrounded.

Eventually, Fargo reached a point a stone's throw from the barn. He was about to sprint across the open space to the wide doors when a man in a hood came out of them, moving furtively. The night rider ran toward the woods, zigzagging to make himself hard to hit. But no shots came from the house.

The man entered the trees not five yards from where Fargo was lying. A few long bounds, and Fargo slammed the Henry's stock against the burlap hood. Not once, not twice, but three times, and at the third blow the night rider's knees turned to butter and he collapsed without a sound.

Fargo swiftly removed the hood. It was big enough and baggy enough that he could pull it on over his head, hat and all. The eyeholes had to be adjusted. Then, the Henry under his arm, Fargo raced toward the barn, zigzagging as the night rider had done. Again, no shots boomed. He darted between the double doors and nearly collided with a night rider already there.

"Harve? Is that you? What are you doing back so

soon? You were supposed to tell Kutyer we saw Glenn Handy at an upstairs window."

"I'm not Harve." Fargo started to raise the Henry to give the man the same medicine he had dispensed to the night rider in the trees, but a cough from deeper in the barn stayed his intent.

Two more night riders emerged. "Charlie says it's as still a cemetery in there," one remarked.

Fargo took a gamble, hoping the hood disguised his voice enough to fool them. "Charlie?"

One of the night riders jerked a thumb overhead. "He's keeping an eye on the house. A bird's-eye view, you might say."

Fargo glanced up. A figure was framed in the hayloft door. If he had knocked the first man out, he would been shot dead.

"Did the boss send you?" the first man now asked.

"I'm to nose around," Fargo made it up as he went along. "Look for a way to get inside."

"It can't be done, not without being cut to ribbons," the night rider responded. "They have someone at nearly every window."

"Nearly isn't all," Fargo said, and slipped past them and on around the door.

They made no attempt to stop him. At the corner he stopped.

Every last window in the farmhouse had been shot out. In some a few panes remained, but the panes had multiple holes.

One of the windows was directly across from where Fargo hunkered. Time for his biggest gamble yet. Whipping off the hood, Fargo threw it to the ground and hurtled toward the house. He took both sides by surprise. From the barn doors came an oath and a "What the hell?" From the top floor of the farmhouse came a shout. On its heels, almost immediately, came the crack of a rifle from an upstairs window.

The shot missed.

Fargo did not slow down. He threw his arms, and the

Henry, in front of his face, and smashed into what was left of the window. Glass crashed and tinkled. His knees came down, hard. Somewhere near at hand a woman screamed. He threw himself at the floor a split second before a revolver spat flame and lead.

"It's me! Fargo!" he yelled while continuing to roll. "Don't shoot!"

But someone did. The slug thudded into the floorboards inches from his head.

"Don't shoot, damn it!" Fargo hollered. He rolled up against a wall. Pushing onto his knees, he heard the *click* of a gun hammer.

"*No!*" a familiar voice bawled. "He's on our side!"

Warm fingers found Fargo's face. Lips brushed his forehead. "You got here just in time," he said.

"I was out in the hall and heard Glenn Handy holler," Calista said. "Where have you been? How did you get through the night riders?"

Boots and shoes scuffed the hall floor. Into the room streamed some of the farmers and the two striplings, Flate and Dancer. They began asking questions.

Rising, Fargo held up a hand. "Post lookouts at windows on each side of the house. Then bring everyone else here." He amended, "Everyone but the children."

"They're safe in the root cellar," Calista informed him.

It turned out that no one had been killed in the earlier exchange of gunfire. The settlers had seen the night riders closing in and opened fire, dropping a couple. The night riders then shot out the windows and peppered the walls, but only succeeded in wounding two women and nicking one of the men.

"What about Rob Howard and Edgar Rice?" Steve Sherwood asked. "Did they come back with you?"

Fargo kept it brief. The news produced downcast expressions.

"If only they hadn't been so hardheaded and rushed off like they did," Calista remarked.

"More lives we can chalk up to that damned Cole Narciss," John Busby growled.

"There's more," Fargo said. "I've saved the best."

The revelation that Narciss was dead met with whoops of delight. A woman started weeping from pure joy.

So much racket was being raised that a cry of alarm from the front of the farmhouse almost went unnoticed.

Fargo's keen ears heard it but he could not quite make out what was said. Bellowing for quiet, he shouldered through the settlers to the hallway. "Who yelled and why?"

"It's the night riders!" a woman answered.

"What about them?"

"They're attacking!"

20

Fargo ran down the hall. The woman was in a room to the left of the front door. As Fargo reached the doorway, a loud *thump* resounded. Something had struck the door. He thought the night riders might be trying to batter it down until he heard the woman's next outcry.

"They're throwing things!"

She stepped aside when Fargo reached the window. Several shadowy shapes were rushing toward the house. All of them hurled objects, whirled, and vanished into the darkness. Long objects, about as thick as Fargo's arm.

Most of the glass in the window was gone. Fargo poked his head out and jerked it back again before he took a slug. The glimpse was enough. The night riders were throwing tree limbs! Limbs that had been stripped of leaves and shoots. Already a dozen were at the base of the front wall.

"What are they up to?" the woman asked.

Fargo would have thought the answer was apparent. "They're going to burn us out. Go get Calista. And hurry."

More branches struck. The night riders were throwing in relays, three men at a time.

Fargo tucked the Henry to his shoulder. When the next three sprinted toward the house, he was ready. At the blast, the man in the middle pitched to the earth. The other two hurled their branches, then helped the stricken man up and together they retreated.

Calista materialized beside him. "Lori said you needed me."

Quickly, Fargo explained. "Have Glenn and Russ take the front windows upstairs. The rest should take windows on the bottom floor. Send two men up here with me."

"Lickety-split," Calista said, and was gone.

Fargo pressed his cheek to the Henry, but had no one to shoot. His wounding of the night rider had brought the attempt to a halt. Soon spurs jangled, heralding Matt Dancer and Billy Flate.

"Miss Baxter sent us," Dancer said. "She sure is pretty. If I was of a mind to make cow eyes at a female, I'd pick her."

"What do you want us to do?" Billy Flate asked. "Sneak out and pick off those varmints one by one? I'd be good at that. I used to wrestle gators when I was growing up in bayou country."

"What do gators have to do with it?" Dancer asked.

"Once you've wrestled gators, wrestling men is easy. I can take down anything on two legs."

"What about snakes? Can you wrestle snakes?"

"You have snakes between your ears," Billy Flate said.

At that juncture more branches hit the farmhouse. Fargo turned. The night riders were already retreating, weaving as they ran.

"What was that?" Matt Dancer asked.

"They're throwing snakes at us," Fargo said in mild disgust at himself for being distracted.

The pair darted to the other window and peered out. It took them a minute to make out the growing pile.

"Those aren't snakes," Dancer said. "Snakes are wriggly and hiss a lot."

"Those are tree limbs," Flate informed him. "I should know. I've climbed a lot of trees. Maple trees and willows are nice to climb, but not pine trees. Pine trees have sap and it sticks to your fingers and hair, and the next thing you know your ma is shaving you bald."

"Shoot anyone who tries to throw more of those limbs," Fargo directed.

Matt Dancer craned his neck to peer into the night. "Should we warn them first?"

"Shoot first, yell after," Fargo said.

"That makes no kind of sense," Billy Flate said. "What good is a warning if you kill them before you warn them?"

"They are trying to wipe us out," Fargo emphasized. "Every man, woman, and child."

"I get it," Matt Dancer said. "We don't show any mercy. Treat them like they are snakes."

"Will you stop with the snakes?" Billy Flate snapped. "If I hear one more word about snakes, I will throw a fit."

"You wouldn't be so touchy if you had been a snake wrangler, like me," Matt Dancer said.

"There you go again. For two bits I would throw you into a pool of gators. If we had any gators. And a pool."

Another figure appeared in the yard. Fargo fixed a bead but did not shoot. It was one man, walking, not running, and waving a strip of white cloth overhead.

"Look yonder!" Matt Dancer yelled. "Is that a piece of long underwear that jasper is flapping?"

"It could be a doily for all you know," Billy Flate said.

"Where would he get a doily out there in the woods? It's not like they grow on trees."

"Maybe he had it in his pocket."

Fargo lowered the Henry. "Whoever he is, he wants to parley. Cover me. If it's a trick, shoot anything that moves." He added, "Except me."

Billy Flate snickered. "That's plumb silly. We'd never shoot you."

"Not unless it was by accident," Matt Dancer said. "And I haven't shot anyone by accident in four or five years."

Fargo went to the door. He gave the Henry to Calista to hold, and reached for the latch.

"Be careful. They're not to be trusted."

The man with the white flag had stopped ten yards out. He was holding his hands out from his sides to show he was not armed.

His hand on the Colt, Fargo went out. At any moment he half expected the crashing jolt of hot lead, but he was not fired upon. "I thought it was you," he remarked.

"I have an offer to make you," Pyle Kutyer said.

"The only thing we want to hear is you and your men riding off," Fargo replied. "You can't win. Not with the reinforcements I brought from Wet Grass."

"They are not enough," Pyle said. "I have upwards of twenty hellions backing my play. But I'd rather settle this without spilling more blood. So here is what I propose. You and the others throw down your hardware and come out with your hands in the air and we will let you live."

"Are you drunk?"

"You have women and kids. Don't you care what happens to them?" Kutyer asked. "So help me, we will shoot them to pieces, those who aren't burned to death first. Is that what you want?"

"This is your idea of an offer?"

"Make no mistake," Kutyer said. "If you do not accept my terms, none of you are getting out of there alive. There is too much at stake."

"Cole Narciss said the very same thing. He planned all this, didn't he? It's his brainstorm?"

"Your point?"

"Cole Narciss is dead."

Pyle Kutyer was undoubtedly good at poker. He showed no reaction whatsoever. "You expect me to believe that?"

"Send someone to confirm it," Fargo suggested. It had occurred to him that with Narciss dead, the night riders would not get the money they had been promised. They would call off the siege and light a shuck for friendlier climes.

"Who killed him? You?"

Fargo did not answer. There was no need.

"Well, well, well." Pyle Kutyer stared at the ground, his brow knit. Plainly, he was pondering what to do.

To help him decide, Fargo said, "Without Narciss you can't make it work. He had a contact in the army, someone who had been giving him information about the new fort. You might as well take your men and make yourselves scarce."

Pyle looked up. "This does change things. You're right. But not how you think it does. Cole took me into his confidence. I've met his cousin, the one in the army. He'll work with me the same as he did with Cole."

Fargo saw where it was leading, and scowled.

"Fact is, mister, you've done me a favor," Pyle Kutyer said. "With Cole gone, I can step into his shoes. I'm the new top dog. All the money we would have split will now be mine." He chuckled. "Yes, sir. I should thank you."

"You're making a mistake."

"I'm not the one trapped in a farmhouse with a bunch of worthless settlers and females," Kutyer said. "Seems to me if anyone made a mistake, it was you when you broke out of the pen. You should have fanned the breeze instead of helping these yacks."

"They know," Fargo said.

"Who? The people in the farmhouse? What do they know?"

"Not just them," Fargo clarified. "Everyone in Wet Grass knows what went on at the pen. I had the men at the saloon spread the word."

"So?"

"So they won't let you try to quarantine anyone else for smallpox. They won't let you take their property. They will fight you."

"With what? Pitchforks and good intentions?" Pyle laughed. "You're forgetting how gullible they are. They're sheep waiting to be fleeced. I'll tell them Cole was to blame for the doings at the pen, and that I didn't have anything to do with it, or with the night riders."

"You expect them to believe you?"

Pyle snorted. "You give them too much credit. I'll convince them I'm as innocent as a newborn babe, then finish what Cole started. A few years from now, when I'm sitting in my mansion, I'll drink a toast to you for all you did for me."

Fargo came close to shooting him. He glanced at the

white strip, but it was not the truce flag that relaxed his hand. It was eight or nine barely visible figures near the trees, with rifles trained on him.

"I've learned from Narciss. I never leave anything to chance," Pyle Kutyer said smugly. "My offer still holds. Surrender. Throw down your weapons."

"Over my dead body." Fargo turned to go. Nothing more remained to be said. The killing would continue.

"You can't save them, you know," Kutyer said. "The best you can do is keep them alive a while longer."

Fargo's temper flared. He fought an urge to punch Kutyer in the mouth, and keep on punching until Kutyer's face was pulp. "Time is on our side."

"You're hoping help will come?" Pyle shook his head. "I have a man watching the Oregon Trail. Whenever anyone comes along, he warns them Wet Grass has been struck by smallpox, and to stay away. So far the only two who slipped through were Dancer and Flate."

Fargo walked to the door. Calista had closed it behind him, but now she pulled it wide so he could enter. He promptly closed it again so he would not take a slug in the back.

"What did he want?"

Fargo told her, ending with, "Everyone else will be wondering, too. Tell them, and while you're at it, spread the word that they are to shoot any night rider who comes anywhere near the house."

Fargo went into the front room and over to a window. The yard was empty. Squatting, he rested the Henry's barrel on the sill. Minutes crawled by and the night riders did not try to add more branches to the growing pile. He caught sight of several, briefly, huddled in the woods. It was not long after that hooves drummed. Several riders were galloping to the west.

Calista returned. Squatting beside him, she raised her head over the sill.

"Are you looking to get shot?" Fargo pulled her down.

"Where do you reckon those fellows are headed?" she wondered. "It can't be Wet Grass. They would be tarred and feathered."

More hours crawled along on a snail's shoulders. Fargo was mystified. The night riders made no attempt to burn them out. Evidently Kutyer had changed his mind and was up to something else. But what?

Four farmers came downstairs. They got right to the point.

"We're tired of standing around like a clump of daisies waiting for something to happen," Glenn Handy announced. "We'd rather take the fight to the owlhoots."

"The four of us will slip out the back," John Busby proposed. "Once we're in the trees, we'll hunt them down."

Steve Sherwood patted his rifle. "We've spent a lot of time in the forest. We're practically white Apaches."

"No," Fargo said.

Glenn Handy poked a finger at him. "Look here, Davy Crockett. You don't have a wife to worry about. We do. My Glenda must be gnawing on her fingernails along about now."

Fargo could not stop them if they insisted, but he had to try. "We can't afford to lose any of you."

"We know the wilderness hereabouts," John Busby said. "We'll be perfectly safe."

Steve Sherwood flourished an antler-handled hunting knife. "I can't wait to bury my blade in a few."

The drum of hooves off in the trees saved Fargo from further debate. That, and a subsequent shout from Pyle Kutyer.

"Are you awake in there? I'm through fooling around. You have three minutes to give yourselves up. Three minutes to come out the front door with your hands reaching for the stars."

"And if we don't?" someone upstairs shouted.

"In five minutes you will all be dead."

21

The attack was ruthlessly efficient.

First the night riders poured lead into the front of the farmhouse. Not the sides or the rear, only the front. The blistering hailstorm pockmarked the house with more holes than a sieve. The wall was thick, but not thick enough to stop all the slugs.

Fargo and everyone else in the front rooms were forced to hug the floor. He was below a window, lying amid shards from the shattered pane, when a sudden glow spilled into the room, an orange-red light that capered on the ceiling and walls. Rising on his hands, he peered over the sill.

Four night riders were almost to the farmhouse, torches flickering in their hands. Fargo tried to bring his Henry up but had to dive for the floor again to avoid having the top of his head blown off. The riflemen in the trees were shooting at anyone who showed him- or herself.

In a room across the hall a woman wailed, "They're going to burn us out! We have to do something!"

Fargo was dumbfounded when she burst from the other room and lunged at the front door. "Don't open that!"

The woman either did not hear him or chose not to obey. She yanked, and the door was not quite halfway open when several fleshy *thwacks* crumpled her like wet paper. She did not utter a sound or move a muscle after she fell.

Quickly, Fargo gained the hall. A well-placed boot slammed the door shut again, and he threw the bolt.

The volleys outside unexpectedly ended.

Fargo ran to the window. The torches had been flung onto the branches and some of the branches were nurseries of newborn flames. But he was not overly worried. There were not that many branches. The house might not catch on fire.

Then, off in the woods, rose a bellow. Once again the night riders unleashed a withering leaden hailstorm. Once again Fargo had to lie on his belly and pray none of the slugs had his name on them. But none came anywhere near him. Puzzled, he glanced up and realized the shots were peppering the wall at chest height, not any lower. That struck him as so strange that he dared another peek over the sill.

Two night riders were running toward the farmhouse. That was not unusual. But what they held was. Each had one end of a large keg, just such a keg as might be filled with ale. Or with something worse.

Scrambling to his knees, Fargo fixed a swift bead. Slugs ripped into the jamb. Splinters flew, some stinging his cheeks, his ear. But he did not duck down. It was not just his life in the balance. It was everyone's. He centered the Henry's sights on the night rider on the left, and fired.

The man tilted onto his heels and let go of the keg. The other night rider lost his grip and the keg fell. Instantly, Fargo centered the Henry on the second man but the first man he had shot staggered into his sights just as he fired.

The second man used his wits. Crouching behind the keg, he shoved with both hands, spun, and fled. The keg was close enough to the farmhouse that it rolled the last few yards and came to rest against burning branches.

Springing erect, Fargo raced to the front door. "Cover me!" he shouted as he plunged out into the night. Smoke was rising from the keg. He kicked it, thinking to knock it away so the black powder would not ignite. But he was slightly off balance and his other foot slipped. Instead of kicking the keg away from the flames, he kicked it into them.

Letting go of the Henry, Fargo whipped forward and seized the keg around the middle. It was hot, so hot his hands blistered. He had a horrific image of being blown to bits as he turned and ran toward the barn. Lead crackled all around him.

A hissing came from the keg.

Fargo threw it. Exerting every sinew in his shoulders and arms, he heaved the keg of powder at the barn doors.

The night riders behind the doors gave voice to cries of mortal terror.

Whirling, Fargo sought to regain the sanctuary of the farmhouse. He had taken less than half a dozen steps when the world came to an end. The earth seemed to rise toward the stars as a wall of invisible force slammed into him and tossed him like a leaf in a tempest. His ears became throbbing pools of agony.

Fargo was not aware of striking the ground. Blackness engulfed him. Blackness so complete, that he lost all sensation, all sense of being alive. The first inkling he had that he was not fit for a pine box came when fingers plucked at his shoulders and someone began dragging him. Dimly, he heard his name, uttered in frantic whispers. Rifles and revolvers were booming and cracking, but so faintly that they sounded like firecrackers. That was when he realized the person dragging him was shouting, not whispering.

The explosion had done something to his ears.

Rousing, Fargo tried to stand, but his legs would not support him. The hands under his shoulders nearly slipped. He looked up, wondering who had braved the hornet's nest to save him. He should have known.

Calista was straining for all her emaciated form was worth.

The courage it had taken for her to rush out was like a bucket of cold water thrown in Fargo's face. He got his legs under him and added his momentum to hers. Somehow they reached the front door. Welcoming arms were flung out to pull them inside. The door slammed shut, but to Fargo it was a dull sound. He leaned against the wall, the world in a whirl. The dizziness did not last. When it cleared and he could think again, he was surprised to find that someone had shoved the Henry into his hands.

Calista filled his vision. She gripped his shoulders and shook him. "Can you hear me? How badly are you hurt?"

"I'm all right," Fargo answered her seeming whisper, which was true as far as it went.

"There is blood coming out your ears," Calista said.

"I'm fine," Fargo insisted. "Give me a minute to catch my breath."

"Take as long as you want. They've stopped shooting."

As unsteadily as a drunken riverman, Fargo lurched to the window. In his stupor he nearly blundered in front of it. A tug by Calista saved him.

"What are you doing? Show yourself and they will shoot you to pieces."

Fargo was listening. The shooting had, indeed, ceased. Gradually, the ache in his ears lessened. He could hear again: whines and sobs from the vicinity of the barn. He went to a side window.

The double doors were a shambles. The left was gone except for its hinges, and the upper two-thirds of the right was missing. Part of the barn had gone up in bits, leaving a gaping, jagged cavity. Bodies sprinkled the grass. In some instances, parts of bodies. A night rider with half his face gone was blubbering and flopping about like a chicken that recently had its head separated from its body.

"Help me, Pyle! For God's sake, help me!"

The plaintive cry reached Pyle Kutyer. There came a shot, just one, and the man who had lost part of his face lost a lot more: his life. He died noisily, weeping and thrashing.

"It will be a while before they try to use a keg of powder again," someone in the room predicted.

Suddenly remembering the burning branches, Fargo

moved as fast as his still wobbly legs allowed to the front window. He need not have worried. The branches were gone. The blast had done to them as it had done to him, scattering them like twigs in a storm, and snuffing the flames.

Calista brought Fargo a glass of water, which he was glad to drink to soothe his dry throat. As he hunkered there by the front window, the woods resounded to the sound of an ax biting into wood. The night riders were chopping at a tree. Their purpose perplexed him. They might use the tree as a battering ram, even though the defenders were likely to make wolf bait of anyone who tried to batter the front door down. The only other purpose he could think of was for the night riders to lean the tree against the house so they could gain entry to the second floor. But with all the upstairs windows covered, the threat was slight.

"Can you hear me in there?"

The shout caused everyone in the front room to stiffen. Fargo answered with, "What do you want now, Kutyer?"

"To give you one last chance to give up. On my word of honor, those who do won't be harmed."

Fargo deliberately laughed long and loud.

"I don't blame you for not trusting me," Pyle Kutyer said. "So how about if I send in a hostage as proof?"

Instantly suspicious, Fargo demanded, "Come in alone and unarmed, and maybe I'll believe you."

"And be shot down by the settlers? No, thanks. I was thinking of one of my men."

Calista leaned close to Fargo to whisper, "If he is sincere, we can get the children out."

"What do you say? I send a hostage, and anyone who wants to light a shuck is free to do so."

"Send your hostage," Fargo said.

"Give me a couple of minutes," Kutyer shouted. "We'll draw lots to see who it is."

A meeting resulted. Glenn Handy summed up the sentiments of most when he remarked, "I don't trust that coyote any farther than I can throw my Glenda, and she's on the hefty side."

"Keep your guns on the hostage from the moment he leaves the woods," Fargo directed. "I want two men at each upstairs window. You can see better from up there. If it's a trick, give a yell."

A commotion was taking place in the woods. Night riders were converging from various points around the farmhouse. Fargo spotted several but did not shoot. He used the lull to replace spent cartridges in the Colt and the Henry.

Reddish-orange light appeared amid the trees. The night riders had started a campfire.

"Look at that," Calista said. "They must be sincere about the hostage or they wouldn't make it so easy for us to see them."

Fargo was skeptical. Yes, the fire revealed a few night riders, but they were far enough back in the trees that it would take a marksman to hit them.

"Someone should fetch the children from the root cellar," a woman named Penni said.

"Not yet," Fargo countered. "Not until we're sure."

The night riders took a lot of time to cast their lots. Just when Fargo was about to shout to Kutyer and demand to know why it was taking so long, a night rider on horseback came out of the woods.

The animal came toward the house at a walk. The man had his arms out from his sides to show he was not up to anything.

"He's not armed," Calista said.

Fargo left the window and hurried to the front door. He opened it enough to see out without being seen.

The horse was a third of the way to the house when it abruptly stopped. The night rider made no attempt to goad it on. Neither his arms nor his legs moved. Yet suddenly the horse gave a start and came on again.

Fargo's eyes narrowed. The rider had not used his spurs or flicked his reins. No one had smacked the animal on the rump. The only explanation for the start the animal gave was if someone had thrown a rock or a stick at its backside. But why would anyone do that when it might have spooked the animal into trotting off?

The night rider came closer. His arms, Fargo noticed, were unusually stiff. So was the man's body. The hands were limp, and the burlap hood was bent low to the man's chest. It was almost as if—

With the thought came certainty. Throwing the door wide, Fargo hurtled from the farmhouse. He raced toward the horse. A shot pealed from the trees. Then another. Both missed. He reached the horse and grabbed the bridle. The reins were wrapped around the saddle horn, not in the rider's hands. The rider could not have held them even if they were; the man was dead, slain earlier in the night, as a dark stain on his shirt testified.

Fargo wheeled the animal around. In doing so he glimpsed the poles that held the corpse upright. One had been shoved down the man's back, under his clothes, the other along the man's arms. But it was the object lashed to the saddle behind the dead man that filled Fargo with dread.

Crackling and hissing, the fuse to the keg of powder was half gone.

With a loud shout and a hard blow, Fargo sent the horse trotting toward the trees.

Cries of alarm came from the woods.

"Shoot the damn horse!" Pyle Kutyer roared. "Don't let it reach us!"

Whipping the Henry to his shoulder, Fargo sprayed lead fast and furious, working the lever as rapidly as he could in order to pin the night riders down until the horse reached them. A few answering shots cracked like walnut shells, but not nearly as many as there would have been.

The horse trotted into the timber.

Fargo stopped firing and threw himself flat, his arms over his head. The blast was as powerful as the first one, but he was farther away this time and spared the worst of it. The horse and the dead man and every night rider within range, as well as a sizeable chunk of vegetation, were blown to bits.

Fargo was up while the echoes still rumbled. He bounded toward the woods. A night rider came stumbling out of the undergrowth, his clothes in tatters. Fargo shot him and vaulted over the falling form. Another night rider was on his hands and knees, groping for a rifle. Fargo cored his head.

More bodies and more body parts were bathed in the glow of the sputtering fire. One man, missing an arm and leg, flopped like a stricken fish. Another, pale ribs showing through his shirt, clawed at the sky for deliverance that would not come.

Further in, hooves drummed. The few night riders who had been spared were fleeing.

But not all of them.

Out of the darkness lurched Pyle Kutyer. His hat was gone and his jacket was ripped and he was caked with dust. He did not say anything. The hatred on his face said it all as his hand streaked to his pearl-handled Remington.

Fargo was holding the Henry in his left hand. His right flashed to his Colt. He cleared leather a fraction of a second before Kutyer and fired a heartbeat before Kutyer's shot. Kutyer missed. Fargo did not.

Kutyer took a step back, a new hole in the center of his chest. But he did not fall. Gritting his teeth, nearly dead on his feet, he struggled to steady his arm so he could shoot.

Fargo fired as Kutyer's Remington rose, fired as Kutyer buckled at the knees, fired as Kutyer pitched forward. No more lead was called for.

Settlers were pouring from the farmhouse. Vengeful farmers gave chase to fleeing night riders.

An arm slipped around Fargo's waist. "It's over," he said, suddenly so tired he could hardly stand. He gazed down into a pair of eyes that promised all the rest and recuperation he would need, and then some.

"Come inside," Calista said.

LOOKING FORWARD!
The following is the opening
section from the next novel in the exciting
Trailsman **series from Signet:**

THE TRAILSMAN #307
MONTANA MARAUDERS

Montana Territory, 1860—
Fargo has faced bad odds before,
but this time he has to take
on a whole town.

The Big Strike was a small café behind a new false front
that looked as if a strong wind would rip it away. But
Fargo could smell food cooking, and the smell was a good
one. There were six or eight tables, only a couple of which
were occupied. It was a little early for supper, Fargo supposed, but there hadn't been a meal on the boat that day,
and he was ready for food. He had venison roast that
wasn't too tough, potatoes, and coffee, which was the best
thing he was served. After he finished his meal, he drank
a third cup of coffee and left. He'd find a drink somewhere else.

It turned out to be harder than he thought it would.

There weren't nearly as many saloons in Fort Benton as he'd thought there would be.

"Drinks are scarce around here because of Sundown," said an old-timer Fargo stopped to ask where the nearest saloon could be found.

"What's Sundown got to do with anything?" Fargo asked.

"That's Whit Anders' town." The man gave Fargo a quizzical look from beneath his bushy brows. "You ever hear of him?"

"I've heard a thing or two."

"I can tell you plenty, but talkin' makes me mighty thirsty."

"Take me where I can get a drink, and I'll buy one for you," Fargo said.

The old-timer, who said his name was Buck Terrell, led Fargo to a place called the Silver Slipper. As they walked through the town, Fargo thought he saw Possum slink into an alley, but when they got there, no one was in sight.

Fargo shrugged it off. Fort Benton was still a small town. Possum was as likely as Fargo to be looking for a place to eat or a place to drink.

"Here it is," Buck said. "The Silver Slipper."

It was nothing more than a shack on the outskirts of the town. As far as Fargo could tell, there was no silver around, and there were for sure no slippers. The place was small, crowded, and smoky. No women could be seen.

"Anders has got most of the women, too," Buck said. He was short, bewhiskered, and wrinkled. His old black hat looked as if a buffalo had chewed on it. "If you know what I mean."

"You were going to tell me about it."

"Better get us a drink first. I'll have a whiskey."

Fargo bought a bottle at the bar and took it and a couple of fly-specked glasses to the table Buck had claimed. He sat down and poured the first drinks. Buck knocked his back and wiped the back of his hand across his whiskery mouth.

"Ah, that hit the spot. Fill 'er up again."

"Tell me about Sundown," Fargo said, moving the bottle out of Buck's reach.

"You're a hard man." Buck eyed the bottle hopefully, but Fargo didn't relent. "All right, it's like this. Whit Anders has robbed and kilt more than his share of folks over the years, and he's spent a lot of time hidin' out in the Missouri Breaks. Some other desperadoes were doin' the same, and before you know it, there was a sort of a town out there. Not exactly a law-abidin' one, either."

He pushed his glass forward, and Fargo poured him a drink. When Buck had swallowed it, he continued.

"Don't need much law in a place like that. Women, whiskey, maybe somethin' to eat now and then—that's what you need. Anders liked the setup, and he got the idea that he'd make himself the law there, except, like I said, there ain't much law. Anders runs the place, and he makes the people who come there pay him if they stay. They have to pay for the hotels and liquor and women, too. And speakin' of liquor . . ."

Fargo gave Buck another shot of whiskey, which Buck downed immediately.

"Thanks. Well, another thing Anders likes is havin' it so that the people comin' into Fort Benton have to go to Sundown if they want to get 'em a woman, or do any gamblin', or have a good drink. Speakin' of which . . ."

He pushed the glass forward again. Fargo took a swallow of his own drink before he poured for Buck.

"I see what you mean about a good drink," Fargo said. "This isn't one."

"Best you can get here." Buck picked up his glass and tapped it against the table. "I ain't complainin'."

Fargo poured, and Buck went on with his story.

"Folks around here don't like Sundown, not one little bit. They don't like havin' a town full of outlaws that close by, and they've tried to close it down. Ain't had no luck, though. Who's gonna go up against Anders and a town full of killers? I guess Stuver's crazy enough to do it, but he can't get hardly anybody to go with him."

"Who's Stuver?"

"He's the town marshal here in Fort Benton. Rex Stuver. Not much of a lawman, but he can keep order. Hell, it's easy for him. Ever'body's scared he'll shoot 'em if they don't do what he says."

"He sounds as bad as Anders."

"Not quite. The difference is that Stuver's a fella who goes by the laws on the books. People can understand that. It's people like Anders and that bunch in Sundown they're afraid of."

"But they won't go in and shut the place down."

"Didn't I just say they're afraid? There's no profit in goin' after Anders. He'd kill you slow and painful if you crossed him, and he'd enjoy it, too. That's the way they do things in that town of his."

Thinking about Sundown reminded Fargo of Possum and Snake. He wondered if they might have been headed in that direction. They seemed like the kind of men who'd be right at home in Sundown.

Buck asked for another drink and got it. The level in the bottle was going down fast, and Fargo had hardly drunk anything at all. That was fine. The liquor was bad, and anyway, he wanted to be sober for his visit later that evening.

"Worst thing of all," Buck said, wiping his mouth, "is that Anders comes to town now and then to raise hell. That's why Stuver was hired, to tell you the truth. Not to keep things in line here but to keep folks safe from Anders. When he comes to town, he takes what he wants. Don't matter to him what anybody says."

"You mean he steals?"

"That's right. Grub, mainly, but he's even took a woman or two. I hear he treats 'em rough for a while, uses 'em and turns 'em over to the madams out there.

They could come back, but they don't want to, not after what Anders has done to 'em."

"And nobody's tried to stop him?"

"Hell, yes. Willie Lawrence did after Anders took off his wife, and look what happened to poor old Willie."

"I wasn't here," Fargo reminded Buck, who was getting a little drunk and maudlin by this time.

"Well, it's just as well. Wouldn't have been anything you could do about it. Nobody did anything about it. That's what was wrong here. Even somethin' as bad as that couldn't get people riled up enough to go after Anders. Except for Willie. He went after him, the poor bastard."

Buck pushed his glass forward. Fargo refilled it.

"It was Hap Tolliver who went by Willie's place a couple of days later," Buck said. "There was a wooden box sittin' on the front porch. Two or three old cats was sniffin' around the box and lickin' at the sides. Hap opened it up and like to died hisself when he took off that lid and saw Willie's face lookin' back up at him." Buck took a drink. "That's when the town got together and hired Stuver."

"Has Anders been back since then?"

"Not yet, but he will be. That's his way. He'll be tired of Willie's wife by now and wantin' somebody else, so he'll come lookin'. He ain't scared of this town. He ain't scared of Stuver. He ain't scared of the devil hisself."

It was an interesting story, and it sounded to Fargo like the town of Fort Benton might be in for some tough times. But it wasn't the Trailsman's problem. He was going back to St. Louis to find another job as soon as the *Chippewa* pulled away from the dock.

A good part of the evening had passed, and the bottle was just about empty, mostly Buck's doing. Fargo didn't mind. Listening to the old man talk had been as good a way to pass the time as any, and better than most.

"It's getting late," Fargo said. "You can have the rest of the bottle."

"Mighty kind of you," Buck said, reaching for it. He might have been slightly drunk but his hand was steady. He held the bottle up to the light and shook it.

"Not much left."

"It'll have to be enough," Fargo told him.

"I'll make do. You gonna be around town for a while?"

"Leaving tomorrow," Fargo said, rising.

"Well, you take care, you hear?"

Fargo said he would and left the Silver Slipper, thinking that it was time for him to pay his visit.

He'd taken no more than a couple of steps outside the door when something slammed into the side of his head and knocked him sprawling.

No other series has this much
historical action!

THE TRAILSMAN